LYNNE O'SULLIVAN was born in Ashford. She worked as a personal assistant before training as an actress. Lynne has written and appeared in several plays. Her thriller, The Refuge was staged in London in 2020.

Gloria

In Extremis

LYNNE O'SULLIVAN

Matador
9 Priory Business Park,
Wistow Road, Kibworth Beauchamp,
Leicestershire. LE8 0RX
Tel: 0116 279 2299
Email: books@troubador.co.uk
Web: www.troubador.co.uk/matador
Twitter: @matadorbooks

ISBN 978 180046 453 7

British Library Cataloguing in Publication Data.
A catalogue record for this book is available from the British Library.

Printed and bound in Great Britain by 4edge Limited
Typeset in 12pt Minion Pro by Troubador Publishing Ltd, Leicester, UK

Matador is an imprint of Troubador Publishing Ltd

Berk on the Sea

Tried to drown myself this morning – no luck obviously, otherwise I wouldn't be sitting here in bed. I'd turned everything off and tidied the kitchen in case people came back for a sherry after the funeral. I wouldn't want them to think I was a slut as well as a complete failure – correction – a fifty-year-old failure. I drove to Hythe at 6a.m. all prepared, but it's hard to drown when you're a good swimmer. I got medals for it at school. Dad thought it was great and even Mum was impressed. *('Oh, you're good at something then, heaven be praised.')*

Once I got into the sea, I planned to swim and swim until I could swim no more and just went under. There was nothing to turn back for – even a brain as slow as mine could work that out. I set off and was doing quite well until that speedboat went by. Its ripples went right over my head and dragged me backwards. I thought, bloody hell – do me a favour, I'm trying to drown myself here!

I'd sort of lost it by then and just bobbed about like a complete tosser. It was bloody freezing too. The wind was gale force – more like December than June. I couldn't see a thing let alone drown myself. I hadn't taken my goggles, not thinking I'd need them. God knows how I got back to the shore with my eyes stinging like hell. When something touched my leg I hoped it was only seaweed and not the remains of someone else with the same idea who'd actually seen it through.

On thinking though, if I had gone through with it there might have been repercussions. I mean, what if I'd floated back to the shore afterwards and some kid had found me? They might have been damaged for life at the sight of me lying there in my black and white cozzie, like that whale they couldn't shift – face all puffed up – well, more puffed up than usual. On the other hand, my huge body could've been blown out to sea and ended up in a trawler net off France – catch of the day – a bloater hauled in with the crabs.

I fell arse-over-head on the shingle and my cozzie was full of pebbles. Some old bloke with a Jack Russell dog was sizing me up as I shook out my crotch. I thought the next bloke to size me up would be the undertaker. I heard that in a film once and pissed myself, never dreaming it would ever apply to me.

'Well done, that girl!' he yelled – ex-military from his salute. You get a lot of them in Hythe. He obviously assumed I'd just gone in for a dip – silly old sod. I tried to hurry away but it was hard getting my flip-flops back on with soaking wet feet. His stupid dog barking and circling me all the time didn't help. I really had to grip with my toes to walk. My bloody trousers had blown right up the beach. The old guy sprang into action, spearing them with his stick before they could take off again. He stood there staring while I yanked them on. 'All present and correct?' he said.

I ignored him and staggered off across towards the car. Luckily, my key was still in the zip pocket. Once inside, I got my cozzie off somehow. It wasn't easy with him at the window twirling his moustache – eyes on stalks. My bum cheeks were probably the most exciting thing he'd seen since Suez. He gave me another salute as I drove off. I felt like giving him one back – the middle finger variety – but I didn't. What the hell was he doing on the beach so early anyway? Some people!

I passed by that sign on the way out of Hythe which twins it with 'Berck-Sur-Mer' in France – "Berk on the Sea" – me, a few minutes earlier. If I hadn't been so cold and miserable, I would've laughed out loud. I thought about going on to Folkestone and seeing Mum for any tiny scrap of comfort that might be on offer till I remembered we weren't speaking.

'Hooray,' she'd said when she found out Roy had left me for someone else. 'Bloody good riddance!' She didn't appreciate he was the love of my life. She'd be bound to quiz me over what I was doing there so early in the morning, knowing it had something to do with him. George would probably be home, anyway. Pity Mum went off on that cruise to find herself and found him instead. If he hadn't sung in the cabaret that night, she might never have laid eyes on him. 'Just like Dean Martin,' she said, all gooey-eyed when she got home – more like a pub singer from the video she'd made. He said when he saw Mum he nearly went overboard. Pity he didn't.

I suppose she sees George as a kind of toy boy, even though he's in his sixties. Mum doesn't look seventy-two, being petite and always well-turned-out. I reckon she could've done better than going for the first bloke on that ship who paid her any attention. She might've aimed for the captain at least, not short-arsed George in his cowboy boots which he wears for added height. As for that habit he's got of pushing his hair back every five minutes – that's just plain weird. I gave it a yank when he hugged me that time just to check it wasn't a "syrup". It was easy enough as he only comes up to my chin. He'd probably try and hug me again if he thought I was upset. No, I definitely wasn't up for George this morning.

I could've gone to Bev's for a hot shower saying that mine was on the blink, but I couldn't remember if she was working today or not. Probably not a good idea, anyway. She might be my sister but there are sides of me she doesn't understand, let's face it. I didn't want to start booing in front of the kids or Darren so I just drove back.

I wanted to keep my suicide attempt (failed) from Alison. That's the trouble with living across the street from your best friend. I knew she'd have something to say about it, like I'm off my game and men in white coats would be after me. It's a stupid saying that – way out of date like "More tea, Vicar?" or "Ooo, matron!". As if there's a budget for specially trained, white-coated men to go around picking up the mentally ill (not that I am) and whizz them off to the nearest "loony bin". Come to think of it, "loony bin" is probably out of date too, like "funny farm" and more than likely non-PC.

Alison just happened to be giving her wheelie bin a wipe as I pulled up. Typical! I tried to sneak indoors without her seeing me but no such luck. As expected, an interrogation followed. I said I'd just been for a dip but of course she knew there was more to it. 'Why on earth did you go in the sea?' she asked. 'It gets rough down there. You could've drowned.'

I confessed that was the object of the exercise. She told me to get a grip and I had no more intention of topping myself than she had or I would've done it by now and as predicted, it's time I moved on from that imbecile Roy. It's all right for her, she's never been dumped by a partner of ten years or dumped at all come to that. I burst out crying then. I couldn't help it. Everything just came to a head.

Alison looked around in case any Newtown neighbours were watching and told me to pull myself together and get indoors. She meant her flat as I'd told her I'd switched everything off here. She said she'd do me some breakfast while I had a shower. I followed her in like a lost sheep, sniffing.

I hate that bloody flashy bathroom of hers. The bloomin' shower's made for hobbits – not great when you're built like a cave troll. I couldn't change the height of the spray for a start, so I had to shower with my knees bent. I stubbed my big toe getting out – it throbbed like hell. The floor was soaked. It took ages to mop up but I couldn't have left it like that. Alison would have freaked. She asked if I tried the massage head as it was so relaxing – very funny.

I dried my hair at her dressing table (also titchy – my knees were under my chin). In the mirror my face looked like one of those Conky balloons that were around when I was a kid – white with a red nose. I remember that time I blew one up and let it go farting round Auntie Kit's living room. I got a right old telling-off for that. Then there was the time Bev and I went to tea and I let another Conky off. It disappeared off the face of the earth until we spotted it up on the lampshade half an hour later. We peed ourselves laughing. Bev choked on a Wagon Wheel and spat it all over Auntie Kit's tablecloth. I can't believe I was laughing over Conky this morning. It just goes to show how that balloon still has power to amuse after all these years, despite the odds.

Alison was full of sound advice over breakfast, telling me to keep my chin up (that was the mistake I'd made in the sea earlier – if I'd kept it down after the speedboat passed, I might be halfway to Boulogne by now) and how about we go to Majorca for a week in September? It was nice of her but I know it's "a sprat to catch a mackerel" as Auntie Kit would say. She met that bloke, Joe, out there a few months ago and has been keeping in touch with him ever since. She calls him José – God knows why when he comes from Dartford. Bit of a playboy I reckon, but she really likes him. He's got a gleaming white villa and teeth to match – I've seen photos. He's also got a private beach, apparently. I said OK, I'd go but I'm not staying at the villa like a prize gooseberry. Turns out Alison isn't staying there either but there's a hotel very near it – a four-star called the Don Quixote. I don't mind a four-star. Fives are too expensive and they don't like sandy feet. If you can't chill out, what's the point? Anyway, I suppose the trip will be a change from staying in and watching films, which is basically all I ever do these days.

First thing tomorrow I'll move my bed so it isn't lined up with the dressing table mirror. OK, I survived the terrible drowning this morning, but I don't need to be reminded of the fact that I'm still around. What a sight! Talk about *Nightmare on Newtown* – dark stick-out hair, big white face and glasses. I look like a kid has drawn me – "The Picture of Gloria Grey". If only I could be rubbed out and re-drawn or better still, rubbed out altogether.

Reflections

Went shopping with Alison today for holiday stuff. Even though we're not going till September she wanted to make a start. She always goes in for the designer range, while I check out the sale rails. Everywhere you look, clothes are being advertised by stick-thin models with goldfish pouts and "bed" hair. I tried on a dress, which as expected was too small. I got my head stuck in the neck hole and when I struggled to get it off, I heard it rip. I had to call Alison from the next cubicle to help. When she saw me she burst out laughing and crossed her legs to stop from peeing. She said I looked like a serf in the stocks. I said it was all right for her, built like a skellington. She said it's *skeleton* and God knows how I've worked in a solicitor's office all these years. I looked it up later. She's right but I could have sworn. It's not a word you come across very often in conveyancing unless perhaps you have to type a report which says *"a skellington has been found in the basement of a property, therefore, the vendor is prepared to come down in price"*.

I got lipstick on the dress too – Scarlet Flush. It was a tester out of Alison's work case. God knows how she makes a living selling make-up at those prices. She said I need to stop wearing so much black by the way – it's like I'm in mourning. I said, 'well I am, aren't I?' Of course, she told me to get a life. Anyway, black is slimming as everyone knows. I ended up getting a bright pink sarong with a cat's face on just to keep her quiet. It was in the sale bin for three quid. She said it was a start, despite being "somewhat garish". I said, 'Thanks a lot.' Then she went on about thinking positive and maybe wearing some slimming lingerie underneath my clothes and had I thought of spandex? Thought of it? How could I forget it? I told her the mere word brought back painful memories of that sixties-themed wedding reception I'd gone to with Roy a few years ago. I was determined to wear that fitted black and white dress I'd got from the charity shop – hence buying the all-in-one body shaper. It stretched down to my thighs and looked like an old-fashioned swimming costume (men's). OK, it had given me a bit of shape – a fat hourglass rather than a storage cylinder – and I looked less like the Michelin tyre man than usual but boy, did I suffer. I remember dancing to "Rubber Ball" by Bobby Vee, feeling like a rubber ball myself when I slipped on some trifle and went skidding along the floor. The bridegroom (sloshed) had helped me up. Just my luck the band had gone off for a break and "Saturday Night's Alright" was playing. Being a big Elton John fan, he was dancing around me, playing air piano and singing at the top of his voice.

It was far from all right actually. It was the worst night of the week as far as I was concerned. At one point I thought I might have to go to A & E to have the body shaper surgically removed. When I finally peeled the bloody thing off I exploded with trapped wind and suction – a lethal combination.

Alison was screaming by this time and asked why hadn't I mentioned this before and it was the best laugh she'd had for ages. I obviously come in useful sometimes.

In the store café I had a hot chocolate with marshmallows and sprinkles and a chocolate penny on the side. I could see Alison was bursting to say something about it but I told her that fifty-year-old mooses (or is it meese?) abandoned by their mates were entitled to eat what they liked. She said hadn't I heard? Fifty's the new thirty. As she's only forty; that makes her twenty – great! She said not to worry as I would always be five in my head. I wasn't sure what she meant by that but didn't pursue. She said I needed to get back on the circuit. I said, "How? Stick my fingers in a socket?" She suggested a class. Maybe a French refresher as I was good at the language at school. Yeah, that's true. I could translate Berck-Sur-Mer at least. Thinking about it, I could have gone on to do A-level French but Mum said cookery would do me more good. How I'd hated those bloody classes! I got partnered with an Italian girl, Angelina something, who had no sense of humour. I remember she used to hog the oven space and call me "weird" without any explanation. Afterwards, the teacher would make us all try a sample of what we'd cooked while the rest of the class watched. I told Alison about the time I made stuffed eggs topped with parsley and felt such a fool when I took a bite and the yolk popped out onto the table. Everyone pissed themselves, of course. I think my role as the class clown began that day.

That was all Mum's fault, but I suppose she was trying to be practical. Cooking never let you down, she reckoned. Roy did though. What about all the tasty meals I put in front of him over the years? Yeah, I should have stuck with French. I could have gone on school trips. I might've met a sophisticated older man over there with a stubbly chin who puffed on Gauloises all day and called me *Ma petite* (even though I'm not). I could be living in a French chateau somewhere by now, with an apartment in the Champs Elysées and never have met Roy in the first place.

'Gloria, are you listening?'

I realised Alison was speaking.

'Sorry. What?'

'I said, staying in all the time watching films isn't healthy.'

'OK, OK, I get it,' I said. 'I'll check out the French classes, all right?'

I won't, of course.

That chocolate penny was delicious. I bit right into it so I had a choccy tooth either side of my mouth like a bulldog. When I growled at Alison, she said see what I mean about being childish and had I forgotten I was lactose intolerant?

I told her I hadn't, actually, but was taking a day off from it if she didn't mind. Sometimes I think she missed her vocation and should've been a headmistress. Boss, boss, bloody boss.

'Suit yourself,' she said.

A few minutes later I was sloping off to the ladies with my tum rolling. That's the annoying thing about Alison – she's always bloody well right.

Thickhead

I passed by the old house today. Ten years I lived there with Roy. We moved in during the summer of 2009. God knows why I keep torturing myself by going anywhere near it. I should've moved away from Newtown altogether, but I grew up around here and I'm fond of the place. Uncle Jack worked in the railway and Auntie Kit still lives across the green. She's always got a story about how Newtown used to be when she was young. Alison says it's not called Newtown anymore, and our addresses are just "Ashford" and the postcode, but I still put Newtown so that its existence won't be forgotten just yet.

I moved to this house because Alison lives opposite and it was nice to have her nearby after the break-up. Also, it's cheaper than the last place, having two bedrooms instead of three – an important factor now that I have to find all the rent myself. Not that Roy contributed much. He was always waiting to be paid and then somehow nothing, or very little, would materialise. I used to say it was OK, even though sometimes I was really stretched.

I stood by the gate remembering my first suicide bid after Roy left – death by washing line. It was only supposed to be a dummy run to see whether the washing line could take my weight – it couldn't. Being the dummy, I found this out the hard way after I'd tied it to the bannister, slipped off and crashed down onto the phone table. The bannister pole descended shortly after, clobbering me on the head. It was like a cartoon; I saw stars and heard birds tweeting.

I wimped out there too if I'm honest. If I'd really meant business I'd have gritted my teeth, put the washing line around my neck instead of my waist and jumped. Instead, I'd dithered about, playing for time, looking out the window trying to imagine how it might feel never to see the street outside again or anything again come to that. It was then that I'd slipped. I probably should have taken my socks off first really.

I blame that bloke posting leaflets across the road. He caught my attention for a second and I lost balance. The crash sounded like the roof falling in. I lay there among bits of table – its legs were busted and splayed out in four different directions. Even though it was a phone table, I never had a phone on it as such. My mobile wasn't handy either. If I'd seriously injured myself, I'd have just had to lie there for days in my own wee and poo waiting to be rescued. How embarrassing for both me and the poor paramedics concerned. Still,

I suppose they must be used to that and just turn a blind eye, or nose rather. The bloke had reached my letter box by then and a leaflet floated down onto the mat advertising home decorating services – well timed but too expensive. I had to do a patching-up job myself before I left the place, blaming deathwatch beetle for the missing bannister. I don't think the landlord believed me though as I never got my deposit back. I suppose it was a silly thing to do really. I could've killed myself.

That was due to Roy of course – all those years wasted. Looking back on how we met, it was sheer chance I'd gone into the County Hotel that Friday night with the work gang – not that we were all mates. Everyone has their little clique at the office and just like at school I've never belonged to one. I think I just tagged along that night for something to do. Little did I know, love was just around the corner! Roy was slumped at the bar with his head all bandaged and a plaster over his nose. I asked him if he'd been in an accident. He looked really depressed and said, 'Sort of.'

I told him he looked a bit like Ronnie Wood, which cheered him up because he could see himself in the mirror behind the bar and thought he looked like Frankenstein. I bought him a drink and he told me how his wife, Sally, had kicked him out earlier when she'd found texts from that Swedish vet Dagmar on his mobile. He was driving taxis then and had left the phone behind by accident. He'd rushed back home for it only to find Sally chucking his stuff out of the bedroom window.

His socks and pants were all over the front garden. He said he'd tried to reason with her but she'd lobbed the phone out then too, donking him on the head. Luckily, it was the Nokia 2332 and not too weighty but it was still heavy enough to do some damage. I couldn't help feeling sorry for him. It was those big chocolate-button eyes of his that got me. I thought they kept crossing due to the pain he was in, but later on I realised they were always like that.

Roy said none of what happened was his fault and that he'd been trying to break it off with Dagmar, who he nicknamed "Dogmar", but she'd clung to him like a limpet. He said Swedes were like that – sex mad. He'd only taken his dog Chalky in with a bad leg and she'd been all over him (Roy not Chalky). He was worried Sally would stop him seeing Tracey and could I run to another drink because the very mention of his little girl's name brought tears to his eyes, which then began crossing even more.

I told him I'd seen loads of cases at work where dads got access to kids no matter what. He said he had nowhere to sleep and none of his so-called mates wanted to know when he'd rung them. He was like a poor stray dog. We went for a Chinese and then back to mine. I got all spruced up in the bathroom, spraying myself with musk, but he'd passed out on the sofa by the time I got back downstairs. He was only supposed to stop the night but ended up staying ten years.

Where has all that time gone? It's been nearly three months now since he went and I'm not really any further on with getting over him. It was an odd relationship but it worked – at least I thought it did. I can't bear thinking of him all cosied up with that bitch Tessa in her posh cottage over in Smeeth. Were there others before her? I don't want to know. All I know is I want him back.

I blame that bloody Alistair actually. If he hadn't got Roy that repping job none of this would've happened. Roy would never have called into that chemist's in Folkestone and met that bitch-clever-clogs bloody man-stealer in the first place. I've always hated Alistair – a real snooty git, he is. It was his bright idea that Roy "turn his life around", meaning he should ditch the taxi driving and become a pharmaceutical rep like him. I was obviously to be ditched as well, only I didn't know that at the time. The taxi-ing went first. Alistair put in a word for him and the next thing Roy was selling drugs around chemists. It obviously didn't matter that he was fifty years old. He doesn't look his age, particularly since he got his eyes fixed. I wished I'd been a fly on the wall at that interview. If Roy was good at anything at all it was talking bullshit. The only drugs he knew about up till then were the ones he took in the seventies when he knocked about with Alistair and his hippy mates in Folkestone. He'd done a massive swatting-up job with Alistair's help. Alistair had made a career out of flogging drugs one way or another since those Folkestone days. Yeah, I blame him one hundred per cent.

I remember the first time we slept together – me and Roy, not Alistair – God forbid. (I once overheard him tell Roy he wouldn't touch me with a dyno rod). He'd been moved in about three weeks. We'd just got back from the pub – I had my old fur jacket on. (I was going to take it to the charity shop the other day actually but I just can't part with it yet.) Roy said it made me look like Bungle off *Rainbow* on TV. I said he was a bit like Emu, the bird puppet with skinny legs who went for Michael Parkinson that time. Things went from nought to sixty when I suggested Emu come upstairs and wrap his skinny legs around Bungle. Talk about a new idea for a kids' show! Haha! Gawd knows why I came out with that but I'd had several vodkas and probably reckoned it was then or never. Roy said it might be like climbing the north face of the Eiger but OK, he'd give it a go – he could be quite romantic when he liked.

I'll always remember that first Sunday morning. It was so nice waking up beside him, even though he said not to get too comfy as it was only temporary. He lit a fag and started twanging his guitar while I got the breakfast ready. That's how Sundays used to be after that – easy and relaxed. Roy got divorced. Life was good. Sometimes we'd take Tracey for a drive down to Folkestone on the weekends that Roy was allowed access. I can't believe she's grown up now with a kid of her own or that Sinbad is getting on for two. We'd take her in the Rotunda and along the beach. Roy would show me all the places he used to hang out when he was young and talk about the bands that used to play at the Leas Cliff Hall and a club called Tofts. There was live music everywhere then, he said. It was sex, drugs and rock 'n' roll and it was a shame I'd missed it. I told him I had fun in my teens too but he just laughed and said, 'Yeah, you might think you did but that was the eighties and a different ball game altogether, love.'

I suppose he was right in a way. I didn't really enjoy myself much back in my teens if I think about it. Mum was always whittling on about where I was going and who with. Dad would be waiting outside the nightclub in his car from eleven o'clock, which was not only embarrassing but really annoying too because, as everyone knows, nightclubs don't start hotting up till then at least.

When I look back, Bev got away with everything on the bad behaviour front. That time she came home paralytic after her work's Christmas do! Bloody hell! Her mates just rang the bell and left me to sort her out. She was in a right state. Lucky Mum and Dad had gone out to a Christmas whist drive and missed the sick in the kitchen sink and in the bucket by the bed. All evidence neatly dealt with by me with the aid of disinfectant and rubber gloves – thanks very much, Sis.

Yeah, Sundays with Roy used to be fun. He seemed content in those days when he was taxi-ing. He was always home by six o'clock during the week. We were happy as Larry – or so I thought. I was delusional, obviously. Thinking back, he must've gone off me (if he was ever on me) and hated me for ages. I was a proper thickhead for not admitting to myself sooner that something was up. He's now a big head showing off in his new life. I remember a cartoon in one of the comics years ago – *Bighead and Thickhead* it was called. That's us, for sure.

Walking out on me after my fiftieth back in March was pretty unforgiveable. I mean, one minute I was laughing my head off dancing to Van Morrison's "Gloria" in the middle of a circle of "friends" (I haven't seen any of them since, apart from Alison) and the next I'm on me tod. Roy waited till the following morning to tell me so that my birthday wasn't spoiled – big deal! I was staggering around the kitchen hunting for paracetamol when he broke the news. I couldn't believe it. I went hysterical. Then, he had the cheek to complain that I ruined his Keith Richards T-shirt by clinging onto him like that and begging him not to go! I mean, what are you supposed to do when your boyfriend walks in and announces he's leaving you for someone else? The more I held on the more he struggled. It's his fault that Keith's mouth got stretched all out of shape like the Moonpig ad, not mine.

One of these days I'm gonna have a look at Bitch Face. I'm gonna drive down to that chemist in Folkestone where she works and see what the fuss is all about. I dunno why I haven't gone before really. Actually, I do. It's because I don't want to be hurt all over again when I find out she's really attractive and it's not surprising I got dumped and what did I expect?

Oh God! I'd get into the bath and slit my wrists like the Romans used to do if I hadn't thrown that rusty old razor out after it scraped my legs to bits. A train's just gone by rocking the house. Come to think of it, that's another possibility – hurling myself from a bridge. I'd have to know what I was doing with that one though. What if I landed on a train roof and went flying up to London? *The Thirty-Nine Steps* gone a bit wrong? How embarrassing to clamber down at St Pancras Station with my hair on end and my legs all askew. They've never been quite right since the phone table incident really. Sometimes my knees ache like hell and I have to rub pain relief into them like an old horse.

Who am I kidding with these suicidal thoughts? It's not healthy, especially when I know I'll never go through with any of them. Why don't I just admit it? I'm an imbecile and a thickhead into the bargain.

Double Whammy

'm still reeling with shock. Today started the same as usual at work with Barnett droning on and on over the tape like someone drifting in and out of a coma. God knows how Sue's put up with it all this time. I have to keep rewinding with the foot pedal to try and fathom what the hell he's going on about. I don't know how he's got away with using that antiquated system all these years. Sue ought to have put her foot down or insisted on not putting it down basically. Then, talk of the devil, Sue herself turns up to show off her baby – a bloomin' huge thing called Henry. She's put on tons of weight and is even bigger than me if that's possible. Her husband's built like a mountain so what chance has the kid got?

Everyone was ooh-ing and ah-ing round the pram, including old Barnett himself which was a bit bloody treacherous. He's hardly said a word to me all the time I've been covering for his darling Sue while she's been off giving birth to Godzilla. Ignorant old git. He was wearing the stretchy onesie I bought him (Godzilla, not

Barnett). I recognised the bumble bee on its collar so I knew it was the one I'd taken to the baby shower. Lucky I got it for a two-year-old. Sue was dubious about its size back then. I said he'd grow into it and now look! She said, 'Yes, who'd have thought?' I was just thinking how Barnett would have to put up with me a bit longer as Sue's not due back till September when things took an unexpected turn.

I should have known something was up when Sue went off to the HR office with her best mate, Donna. They were in there for ages. Just after lunch Donna buzzed me – could I pop down, please? When I got in there she told me to take a seat. It was probably nerves but I nearly laughed out loud as it reminded me of that joke where someone says, "Take a seat" and the other person marches out with a chair. I saw my file out on Donna's desk, recognisable from a Polaroid of me taken ten years ago on the cover. Talk about happier times!

'So, Gloria,' she said. 'You've been with Mr Barnett for six months now and how have you found it?'

I wanted to say bloody awful and the sooner I can get back to being float sec the better but I just said, 'Yeah, great, it's been really interesting.' (Not.)

Talking of Barnetts – Donna's hair seemed to have got bigger and rounder overnight so that instead of a chrysanthemum as usual, it looked like a huge black dahlia – the pom-pom variety. Do dahlias come in black? I've seen them in a very dark red which looks almost black, anyway. It reminded me of a film called *The Black Dahlia* about a nun who went rogue – oh no, that was *The Black Narcissus,* wasn't it? What was *The Black Dahlia* about then? I'll have to look it up.

Donna then announced that Sue was coming back next week instead of September. Apparently Mountain Man (Brian) has had his hours cut (I was thinking he should have something else cut too thereby preventing more Godzillas) and what with the little one (little?) they were finding things a bit of a struggle. She said this in a low voice as if I was being trusted with some sort of special secret. I said, 'Oh what a shame,' but that I didn't mind being float sec again sooner rather than later. Then she started going on about how the new girl, Bina, has done so well standing in for people and covering my reception duty while I've been doing Sue's work. I had to agree – Bina's always got a smile on her face, a diamond in her nose and gorgeous shiny black hair which swings to and fro when she moves, but what did that have to do with me?

'You say you've found working with Mr Barnett interesting,' said Donna. 'But there have been one or two complaints about your abruptness over the phone, Gloria…'

I said, 'Eh? What do you mean?'

'You seem to have forgotten the verbal warning you received a few months ago…'

'I told you I was going through a break-up. I was on my knees. It was sheer luck I made it into work at all!'

Bloody cheek! Why was she dragging all that up again? And there was no confidential voice now, by the way. The whole bloomin' office could probably hear.

'Yes, so you explained. You also said you would try to improve, but you don't seem to have done so.'

I knew who was behind this. That old misery guts Hardcastle, who's got a property sale going on at the moment. He calls every five minutes and is a pain in the neck. He's got nothing better to do all day than keep chasing things up, even though he's probably filthy rich already. Barnett is known for going at his own pace – a snail's, which doesn't help. It's not my fault if things don't move quickly enough. No wonder I often ignore the phone. If I've got Roy on my mind, which I usually have, I just can't be arsed and let it bounce back to the wonderful Bina. If I do bother to answer I might come across as a bit impatient at having my thoughts about Roy interrupted. Lately, if I think I've pushed it a bit too far, I've pretended not to recognise Hardcastle's voice when he's called and put on a BAFTA-winning friendly one, so he'll think I'm someone else and that rude person he spoke to before was just a temp. I'm not very good at acting though, that's the trouble. I've probably been rumbled.

I said, 'If it's Mr Hardcastle, he's a bit deaf and can't make out what I say half the time…'

'Well, Bina seems to manage all right.'

I thought, yeah, she would, wouldn't she?

'Anyway, it's not just Mr Hardcastle,' Donna went

on. 'Others have complained that your attitude when they call is quite unhelpful.'

'Only because they're so bloody rude. Why should I tolerate verbal abuse?'

'Gloria, we've always prided ourselves on having a very good relationship with our clients as I thought you would have known after so many years' service. They expect to hear a cheery voice at the end of the line. We can't afford to bring our personal problems to work, no matter how depressed we might be feeling...'

I went to say something, but she held up her manicured hand to stop me.

'It's not just the clients, I have to say, Gloria. Your colleagues also find you difficult to work with. You don't seem to want to engage or interact. You've always been a little reserved, which is fair enough, but recently you appear rather surly. This doesn't make for a very good working atmosphere.'

'I've never got on well with people here if I'm honest,' I said. 'Everyone's got their own little cliques and I don't fit into one, never have. But that doesn't bother me really. I just like to come in, do my work and go home. I've done that for ten years without any complaints. As for surly, I've never been one for small talk.'

Especially with a bunch of idiots, I wanted to add, but didn't.

'Unfortunately, Gloria,' Big Bonce went on, 'as you may or may not know, the practice is suffering financially for various reasons. We've been asked to shave expenditure wherever possible and I'm afraid this has called for redundancies. The bottom line is that head office has recommended two members of staff to be let go. It's been decided that they will be yourself and Bernard Marshall.'

I just sat there.

'Let go?' I said when I could form a sentence. 'Go where?'

'Let go from the company, Gloria. I'm talking about redundancy in line with recommendations from head office.'

'But surely it's last in first out, isn't it? Bina's only been here a few weeks so how does that work?'

'Bina has a law degree and is regarded as a potential asset to the firm.'

'How am I regarded then, after ten sodding years?'

'This decision has been based on performance and in Bernard's case, age.'

I thought of Bernard sitting at his desk flicking through invoices with his little finger raised. He's bloody seventy, if he's a day, and should've gone ages ago – if you ask me.

'I'm sorry, Gloria. My hands are tied.'

I thought, yeah, they bloody well should be and so should your ankles, mate – hog-tied, that's what you should be, and then roasted on a spit. As for shaving, you should be completely shaved everywhere including that stupid pom-pom bonce of yours and then you should be tarred and feathered like in *Ryan's Daughter* and then you should be…

'Obviously, you'll receive redundancy pay in line with years of service.'

She went on about what I could expect, but I wasn't listening anymore. I was too traumatised. How could they do this to me? She closed my file like I was dismissed. The interview (with a vampire) was over. There was clearly no point in arguing. I was on the receiving end of a decision made by the hierarchy, prompted, no doubt, by Mr Hardcastle. It was all stitched up and probably had been for months. I felt like giving her desk a bloody good kicking, but instead I staggered out, clutching the wall for support. She had the cheek to ask if I was all right when I was obviously on the verge of collapse. When I passed by reception, Bina (legally trained and a total asset to the firm) flashed me her friendly smile. I could've pushed her off her seat. It was so bloody unfair!

Vic was in my office changing a couple of spotlights which had needed doing for ages. News travels fast, especially bad news, hence Vic deciding to sort the lights just as I returned, red-eyed and wobbly, from HR. Vic's probably the only real friend I've had in the place. I go puce even now, remembering how I fancied him like mad when he first joined. All that money spent on my hair and face only to see him in Folkestone one day, arm in arm with another man.

I never quite gave up on Vic though, hoping there was a slim chance he might still like me as I'm quite like a man, too. Well, I could easily pass for one, let's be honest. He said it was a shame they were getting rid of me as I was the company mascot like on *University Challenge* and he reckoned they'd have to find a new one now. Bloody hell! As if that was the only problem with me being shafted! Now I knew how Julius Caesar must have felt after he got stabbed in the back by his so-called chums – or chum in my case (now ex). Well, they can just stick their job up their holes as far as I'm concerned. I'm glad I decided on payment in lieu of notice. I can't face going back there again. When I think of all the work I've done there. Bunch of bloody treacherous bastards!

I called in on Auntie Kit on the way home. She wouldn't have understood about what happened at work of course, or that I was suffering from PTSD, so I didn't say anything. It just helped to be near her somehow. I remember that time at primary school when a boy accused me of stealing sweets from his desk when I hadn't, even though I'd had my eye on them for some time. Auntie Kit had taken me back to school and demanded to speak to the headmistress. It had all been sorted out, but I got no apology as I remember. It was horrible being falsely accused like that, especially by a boy who had dirty nails and smelled of wee. I imagined Kit a few years younger, confronting Donna Big Bonce on my behalf over this latest injustice, which of course is probably another example of how childish I am.

I made a big to-do of filling the kettle and hung

about in the kitchen so that Kit wouldn't see my leaky eyes. I really wanted to put my arms around her and cry into her lap like when I was a kid, but it was risky. I'm a lot bigger now for one thing and she's gone quite tiny – bones might've been crushed. Anyway, she offered me a slice of Battenberg, so that was something.

I told Kit she needed a new kettle – a jug type instead of that old whistle thing she's had for donkey's years. Of course, she said she didn't want anything new fangled and that she knew where she was with the whistle. Just like when I bought her that digital clock to save her from shining a torch on her watch in the night, she wasn't having any of it. How was she to know it wouldn't blow up? Anyway, she said she wouldn't need a new kettle where she was going and would I look after Khrushchev when the time came? She was obviously in one of her funny moods where she keeps talking about not being around anymore. I told her not to be daft, but she made me promise and to be sure that I covered the cage with a cloth at night so the budgie would know it was bedtime. I don't really need a budgie with Mog around, particularly one as unattractive as Khruschev who has barely a feather on his head due to contracting french moult a few years ago. I don't really need Mog either come to that. She's Roy's cat and has gone a bit rogue since he left, spitting her food out on the floor and glaring at me a lot. If I'd had my wits about me, I should have made him take her when he cleared off but of course she wouldn't have been welcome chez Bitch Face – too hairy for a start.

I thought she was losing weight (Kit not Mog, who's quite fat actually) like she's already starting to fade away. When she put her hand on my wrist it was like a feather landing on it. She asked if I'd made up with Mum. She doesn't like it when we quarrel. Being twelve years older than Mum she still looks out for her little sister. Never mind about me and what I have to put up with.

As usual, to justify her concern Kit went on about how Mum was fragile and highly strung like Nana Flo had been and it wasn't her fault when her nerves got bad. Also as usual, she went on about how Bev takes after Mum in build and I'm more like Dad – big-boned, which isn't particularly flattering. I remember Kit once let slip that Mum had been a "mistake" but she never said any more on the subject or about Nana Flo really. Nana Flo is a skellington in the cupboard, that's for sure. All I know about her is that she fell into the river and got pneumonia. There's no point in asking Mum anything about Flo either as she never knew her mother. Flo died from the pneumonia and having Mum at the same time. I reckon that's what must've sent Grandad Alf over the edge and why he went into Chartham Hospital. "That's all he wrote" as they say, except it wasn't actually because I found that note from him in one of Kit's old handbags saying, *Kitty, don't forget eggs – Dad*, done in pencil. It was really faded but I could still just make it out. This was obviously written after Nana Flo had gone and before Grandad went into Chartham when Kit was trying to run the house and look after him and Mum, who was only little.

The last time I talked to Bev about all of this she said an old lady in her nursing home had known Nana Flo when she was young. She'd lived in the same cottages down by the flour mills around the same time as when Flo had nearly drowned. She said it was when the river had burst its banks and there were floods. She reckoned that Flo didn't just fall but chucked herself in and tapped her nose all secretively. The old lady has since passed away but Bev says she was diddle-o and why on earth would Nana Flo have done that? I had to agree it was strange. I remembered doing the life of Virginia Woolf in English lit at school and how she'd filled her pockets with stones to weigh her down when she walked into the river. I said I'd need two concrete blocks which had everyone in hysterics.

Kit started on again about Uncle Jack being around and swore she'd seen him at the bedroom door. I had to hear all about how they'd first met at a dance at the Corn Exchange, even though I've heard it loads of times. Then she said there was something in the understairs cupboard for me, but I couldn't have it until after she'd gone. God knows what she was going on about. As I was leaving she told me again to patch up with Mum and give her a call. I said I would – even though Mum ought to phone me if anything. After all, she started it that day when she found out Roy had been gone since March. She said the only thing we had in common was choosing the wrong men and thank goodness for George as he's the best thing that ever happened to her! That really got me. I said she'd got a bloody cheek and where did that leave me and Bev, not to mention Dad who'd worked up in Cannon Street all those years to provide for us and if the stress of commuting and the heart trouble hadn't finished him off, her bloody henpecking would've done!

That was when she told me to grow up and get out but I can't remember in what order. Oh yes, it was grow up first. 'Gloria, for goodness sake, grow up. You're fifty years old.'

I said, 'Thanks a lot for reminding me. I wish I was dead!'

'Oh, get out!' she yelled.

Charming.

George was coming out of the loo, smoothing his hair frantically just as I got to the front door. I haven't been back since.

I was about to take Kit's recycling down to the bin but she told me to leave it – she'd take it herself for something to do. Then she started on about the gas bill and could I sort it. Turned out it wasn't a bill at all, just a circular but as usual she didn't believe me. She said it would be my fault if she was cut off and why did they take her gas meter out in the first place when she'd saved a whole bottle of shilling bits to put in it?

'Don't be surprised if you find me sitting in the dark next time you come round,' she said. Not only was she muddled about the gas and electric but also which century we're living in.

I did as I was told and called Mum from the car – not to patch up but just to tell her that Kit had been saying daft things about minding the budgie after she's gone and about the gas bill and everything. Mum said Kit's been saying that stuff a lot lately on the phone and did I want to go to tea next Sunday by the way. I supposed this was the olive branch, so I said OK. I didn't say anything about losing my job as she'd only kick off and want to know the ins and outs of a donkey's backside and as usual it would all have been my fault anyway.

I popped into the chipper. My head was all over the place after what happened at work and I couldn't be bothered to cook. As I stood waiting for a cod (large) and chips I thought back to when I used to go in there as a kid for chips with crackling. The fish and chips were wrapped in newspaper then and were called "Fish Suppers". Kit says people used newspaper in the loo in the old days before graduating to that stuff like tracing paper. She still had that paper in her toilet long after tissue became available though. I suppose old habits die hard. That loo paper was hard and no mistake. I wonder if newspaper made people's bottoms black when they used it? Wasn't there a dance called the Black Bottom? Maybe that's where it came from.

Just as I turned the corner into the street here, the second bombshell of the day hit me. Roy was getting out of a fancy new car and walking towards the house! My heart jumped up into my throat. Could he possibly have come back? For one horrible moment I thought the car might belong to Bitch Face and worse still, that she might be sitting in it. If so, she was asking to get a large cod rammed down her gullet whether she wanted it or not. I was determined to stay in control though and took a couple of deep breaths and headed across the road. Unfortunately, I caught my sandal in a paving stone and tripped a bit. I nearly lost all my street cred but just managed to right myself before Roy spotted me. The car was empty (thank God).

'All right?' he said as if nothing had happened. He had on a smart blue suit and his hair was all highlighted and gelled into spikes. Ronnie Wood had been replaced by Barry Manilow. I forgot all about acting cool and had a big stupid grin on my face at the sheer sight of him. I wanted to say it was great to see him and how I'd missed him and about all the pain I've suffered and did he know what he's put me through. In the end I just said yeah, I was OK and if he'd let me know he was coming I could've got him something ready. God knows why I said that. As if he'd come for dinner! I mean, what planet? He said he didn't eat fish and chips – as if that was for peasants. I reminded him that he used to eat it. He said he used to do a lot of things like smoking but not anymore and did I still have his passport because that's what he'd come for.

I unlocked the front door with a dead weight in

my chest and my eyes pricking with disappointment. Why couldn't he have come back to stay? The passport was up here in the dressing table drawer. I prayed he'd realise he'd made a big mistake, follow me up and push me onto the bed for a bit of Bungle and Emu like the old days, but no such luck.

When I went back downstairs he asked why I'd moved here so close to the railway line and what was wrong with the last place? It was pointless going on about memories and economy – he was brain-dead to both. I just told him I needed a fresh start, that Alison lives across the street and Raj's shop is only a few doors up.

I told him I'd tried calling him a few times but he said he'd changed his number, which I thought was a bit hurtful. After all, I only wanted to chat now and then. I asked him about the flashy new car. He said it came with his promotion – bigger territory now and more responsibility. As well as Kent, he'd been given East and West Sussex, Thurrock and the Isle of Sheppey.

I gave him the passport. Turns out he's off to Marbella soon (with Bitch Face obviously). I told him I was going away too – with Alison in September. I reckon he was a bit surprised at me going anywhere without him for a change (ha bloody ha!) but he said I'd need a bigger swimsuit for a start and that I'd piled it on since he last saw me. Bloody hell! The cheek of it! I said he was hardly God's gift himself and that bitch Tessa was gonna wake up one of these days.

'See, I knew you'd be like this,' he said. 'Acting like a big kid as usual. I'm surprised you had to ask why I changed my bleedin' number.'

He was fiddling with the door then, trying to get out, but that lock's awkward if you don't know how to twist it.

'What does she make of your saggy arse?' I said. 'What about your snoring? Not to mention blasting away after a few pints, like the twenty-one-gun salute? How do you get around that one? Lie there with your cheeks clamped together all night?'

He was clearly fuming.

'I told you I watch what I eat nowadays,' he said. 'And I've joined a gym. You should try it yourself sometime. How do you get this fuckin' door open?'

'What about Tracey?' I said. 'Is she proud of having a two-timing git for a dad? I bet she thinks you're a bloody disgrace walking out on me like that!'

'Never mind what she thinks,' he said. 'You keep your ugly fat nose out of my business!'

He said it right into my face with his eyes full of hate. I noticed they were still slightly crossed in spite of the op. Perhaps they were making their way back towards each other in defiance, which would serve him bloody well right. He got the door open then and shoved me out of the way. He was halfway down the path when I grabbed the fish and chips from the hall table and hurled them at the back of his head.

'Bastard!' I yelled. 'You're lucky I don't come over

to Smeeth and put a brick through the window! Some would!'

'Fuck off, you fat cow!' he yelled. Then he got into his car and zoomed off or tried to, but the gears grated and it stalled so he had to start it again and skidded off round the corner. I almost wished he'd have an accident and break his sodding neck.

I collapsed on the doormat. I knew I'd probably never see him again and I'd lost my dinner, too. When I stopped howling I realised it was a shame to waste it and went outside in search. Luckily, no one was about. The mushy peas were a mess on the path which the cat was licking up. There were chips everywhere. I picked a few up and dusted them off. The cod was lying in the grass. I quickly put it back in the box. It didn't taste too bad really.

Pugs and Punishments

finally went to the chemist in Folkestone where Bitch Face works today. I've been calling her "Bitch Face" for want of a better description and decided it was time I actually saw her in person. I mean, "Bitch Face" means the face of a dog, or rather a bitch, so only half of that is right. She had to be a bitch at least, to steal Roy from me, even though of course he was probably guilty of contributing to the offence. As to the "face" bit, that needed clarifying. Female poodles, Pomeranians and Bichon Frises all have nice little faces, even though they're bitches. Every time I say "Bitch Face" I need to be sure what dog, or rather bitch, I'm referring to and see it in my mind's eye.

I knew where the chemist shop was from the paperwork Roy put in the bin the day before he left. He'd got everything planned of course and cleared out the desk he used in the spare room. I had a good old trawl through before the bin men came and found reports of frequent visits to one particular place in

Folkestone where the contact was Ms Tessa Tonkins – a stupid name for a start. Roy's life (and mine) had changed completely just because he happened to call in there one day on his rounds. I tried to push the scenario out of my mind, but I suppose they got chatting across the pain relief and that was it – my own pain was about to begin – with no relief, thanks a lot.

The shop was empty when I got there, apart from the pharmacist and a petite woman with blonde hair working by the till who I took to be Bitch Face. I pretended to be interested in a pair of glasses and turned the carousel, trying on frames while I stared at her. As for dogs, I thought she resembled a Pekingese first, with her tongue poking out in concentration. What with her silly fringe and top knot, she only needed a pink bow to qualify for Crufts. The man-stealing-air-headed-home-wrecker was chatting away to the pharmacist without a care in the world. Fury welled up inside me like molten lava at the thought of her and Roy together. Before I knew it I was hurrying towards her shouting, 'Oi!'

'Can I help you?' she asked.

'Yes, you can actually,' I replied. 'Try keeping your hands off people's boyfriends!'

'I beg your pardon?' she said, all doe-eyed, or rather dog-eyed, innocence.

'Don't give me that,' I said. 'Roy Chislett! Ten years we were together before you got your bloody claws into him!'

'I can assure you I haven't the faintest idea what

you're talking about!' she replied snottily. 'I don't know any Roy Chislett but if he was your boyfriend I'm not surprised he looked elsewhere!'

The pharmacist jumped in then like a ref. 'Ladies, please!' he said. 'Customers may come in at any moment!'

It was then I realised I was still wearing the glasses I'd pretended to be interested in. The price tag was hanging over my nose. I took them off and was just about to give her a bit more verbal when I noticed her name badge read "Gemma" rather than "Tessa".

'Those are thirty-five pounds by the way,' she said. 'If you don't want them, put them back, please!'

I felt myself go red. I chucked the frames down on the counter and quickly went to the door just as another petite female came in. This one had a round face and chin-length highlighted hair pushed back under a band. Her name badge read "Tessa". We did a silly dance as we tried to pass each other, going the same way. I felt like a galleon compared to her – a big galleon with the wind taken out of its sails. She suddenly sneezed.

'Oh, excuse me!' she said, sniffing. 'Hay fever!'

Her eyes were dark and she had a really small nose which was twitching. I ought to have said something. I had the chance, for goodness' sake – she was standing right in front of me, but I couldn't speak a word. I hurried out to the car. I hadn't achieved much at all except to discover that Bitch Face looked like a pug. So what? She still had my man whatever dog she looked like. I drove back to Ashford sobbing.

I knew Alison was shopping in town so I texted could we meet up. I waited for her on a bench outside what was once Woolworths, eating a comforting sausage roll. I remembered when Auntie Kit had worked there on the sweets counter in an overall and cap. She'd always given me an extra bit of fudge when I'd gone in with my pocket money. I bet it was a nice job weighing out sweets all day. Better than bashing away on a PC only to be kicked in the teeth after ten years' hard labour.

When Alison arrived I told her about Folkestone and how I had embarrassed myself big time. I was surprised when I didn't get reprimanded. She said never mind, at least I'd satisfied my curiosity, even though I'd hurled abuse like a fishwife at the wrong person and if anything I should have thanked the pug for taking the useless waster off my hands.

'Look at the trouble he's caused you,' she said. 'It's because of him you've been depressed and lost your job. Was he really worth it?'

I knew the answer, but I didn't feel it. In spite of everything I was still living in hope that he'd come back.

'Talking of which,' she said, 'have you thought any more about reversing things and going for "Unfair Dismissal"? You might well have a case. After all, ten years is a long time.'

'Alison, forget about it,' I said. 'I don't need the aggro. I'm just glad to be rid of the bloody place. I wasn't dismissed; I was made redundant and got a reasonable package. End of.'

'Well, have you done your CV?'

I haven't, of course. I told her the prospect of traipsing around agencies being interviewed by twelve-year-olds did my head in.

'Gloria, it's 2019. This is all done online now,' she said. 'When they get your CV, they'll probably interview you by phone.'

'I'll be very surprised to hear anything back. My CV will probably be deleted right away in favour of one belonging to a much younger, highly skilled person like Bina.'

Of course, she then started lecturing me about being more assertive and having more belief in myself and did the fact that I'd been working since I was sixteen count for nothing? (Probably not.) The sooner I got that CV together the better and she'd be very happy to give me a hand. I said blimey, OK, but could I finish my sausage roll first? (I didn't let on I'd already had one.)

When I got back here I looked up some CV templates so I could tell Alison I'd made an effort at least. Then I opened a bottle of wine and glugged down a couple of glasses trying to forget the business at Folkestone, but of course it was still there in all its embarrassing detail no matter how much I drank. I wish I was articulate and confident so that I could have taken the pug down a peg and flounced out like they do on telly. I hoped I wasn't on CCTV and that I wouldn't get prosecuted for threatening behaviour or potential theft.

I came up to bed around eleven, but as for sleep, forget about it – too much on my brain. I tried counting back from a hundred but did it in no time and am still wide awake. I've just been lying here thinking of all the horrible things that have happened to me over the years – the perpetrators of which have never been punished. If I had my way they'd all be incarcerated in a prison, or correction facility as the Americans would call it – a bit like Alcatraz but not so luxurious – on a faraway beach where the sun never shines. The oldest inmate would be Mandy Cook who abused me when I was seven by yanking down my pants on the green that day. There I was, lying on a blanket in the middle of the grass, reading my comics, when she suddenly decided to creep up behind me, lift up my dress and pull my knickers down over my bum. Thinking about it, she must have been about eight at the time, as she was one class higher than me at school – old enough to know better than to expose my bottom to the entire neighbourhood anyway.

On dishing out her sentence at the beach prison I suppose I'd have to take into consideration that Mandy was still a minor when the crime took place. Her term would've been just eight years – one for every year of her life – had she not reoffended a few days later by eating an entire bar of chocolate in front of me without offering a single bite. It goes without saying that for this grossly serious offence her sentence would be increased to life. Mandy's cell would face out to sea and have no comforts. The punishment would need to fit the crime so I'd dangle slabs of chocolate on a string through a hole in the ceiling just out of her reach. I would wait till the chocolate was nearly within her grasp, then wiggle it about a bit so she could smell it, before reeling it slowly back up to my control room above. As a reminder of her first offence, Mandy wouldn't be allowed to wear pants no matter what the temperature.

Karen Fennell would occupy the next cell. God, was I gutted when she married Steve Coombs who I loved so much in my teens, even though he never gave me a second glance. All the more gutting was that mole on her chin which Steve seemed oblivious to. I mean, I may be on the large side but my skin is blemish-free at least. It's about the only thing I do have going for me. I'd consider shortening Karen's life sentence if she agreed to a replay of her wedding. No doubt she'd be only too happy to have the chance to relive the happiest day of her life except that, unbeknown to her, there'd be a minor change in the proceedings. When the vicar enquired of those assembled if there was any lawful impediment to the marriage, a battalion of my armour-clad guards would rush in protesting that the whole ceremony was a sham and Steve should be marrying me instead. They'd march the struggling Karen away between two rows of upright spears while I took my rightful place beside Steve who, having come to his senses, would smile with relief at having been rescued from a life more moley.

No one would ever know Karen's whereabouts after that except of course me and my guards, who'd be paid so well they'd never let on. Every now and then I would drop food into Karen's cell – just basic stuff like bread, water and the occasional slice of meat. How comforting it would be to watch Karen scuttling about the floor of her cell, dusting sand from bits of chicken and stale bread rolls! During her sentence she would become old-looking and wrinkly. The mole on her chin would have hairs coming out of it (no tweezers or hair-removing cream allowed). Steve would wonder what on earth he ever saw in her if a visit was permitted, which of course it wouldn't be – not even with a window between them and a phone to speak through. No – Karen would have to remain hidden from public view while she completed her sentence, which, despite the wedding re-enactment, would revert back to the life-long term after all.

Another lifer would be Mrs Hales, my needlework teacher. Hating needlework as I did (and still do, let's face it) I was quite happy that she ignored me for weeks at a time but will never forget the afternoon she caught me staring out of the window. She told me to bring my cotton blouse to her for inspection and then made a big show of holding it up, asking whether it was made for Admiral Lord Nelson. OK, so I'd stitched an armhole up by mistake, who hasn't? I felt so stupid when everyone fell about laughing at my expense. OK, I was the class clown, but this was something else. Mrs Hales' cell would face out to sea and get the full blast of the ocean's freezing spray. I like to imagine her getting really excited when I'd lower a basket of cardigans down until she realised that every one of them had a sleeve missing. 'Ha bloody ha!' I'd yell from my control room above. 'You shouldn't have been so quick to show me up! That'll teach you!'

All these crimes were heinous, Karen's in particular, but would I consider parole or bail for any of these offenders? Probably not. OK, Mandy's crime was committed forty-two years ago but would it be fair to release her back into a world that has changed so much since her arrest? It's unlikely she would be able to work a computer or get her head around a mobile phone. She'd be like a fish out of water. No – best to leave her where she is – near to both fish and water.

As for Prisoner Hales, guilty of cruelty towards a pupil while favouring others – an offence that today would warrant instant suspension or even dismissal with her ugly mug appearing in the papers – she will remain in her cell, cold and sleeveless.

In real life Mandy emigrated to Australia and is probably still pulling people's pants down over there; I wouldn't put it past her. Karen is married to Steve with grown-up kids and Mrs Hales is in Bev's nursing home. The funny thing is, Bev says she's always complaining of the cold and asking her to close the window even in the summer. Now that's what I call spooky! Haha!

Tessa's cell would be the worst of all of course, filled with loads of horrible creatures like snakes and rats, a snail or two and a couple of slugs. If she touched the metal bars to the cage she'd get a nasty shock. The cage would be rigged to work like a taser or cattle prod. There would be a toilet – a huge concession on my part considering the gravity of her offence, but it would have no seat, just the bowl. This "privy" would have no privacy as it would be fitted with a camera and a loud siren which would go off every time Tessa used it. In spite of the prison's secret location, any shipping within a five-mile radius would be able to tune in and see her perched on the throne. Tessa's cell would always be partially submerged in the sea so that her feet would be constantly wet. Unlike those salons where goldfish used to nibble the hard skin off your feet, all kinds of fish would have a go at Tessa's, including large crabs and Portuguese men-of-war. She might end up with a case of trench foot like the soldiers in the First World War. Unlike them she'd deserve it.

God, what was that? A car alarm. Great! I was just dozing off at last – thanks a lot! For a moment I thought it was the alarm on Tessa's toilet. Perhaps Alison's right; I should get out more.

Hard at Work

The trouble with sending off CVs is there's always a slim chance of getting employed, particularly since Alison helped put mine together. I wouldn't have had a clue.

I woke up to a loud buzzing noise one morning. I couldn't make out where it was coming from. I thought perhaps a giant bee had got in till I remembered I'd changed my ring tone. It's all part of a new campaign to make changes to my life rather than ending it. I read a motto somewhere that said *"If you can't change the wind, change your sails"* so after I'd moved my bed, I swapped "Meadow" for "Bumble Bee". "Meadow" reminded me too much of Roy. I used to like the sound of birds tweeting, but when he left they sounded more like crows cawing. It reminded me of the times he'd called to say he'd be home late or not at all.

When I forced my eyes open, the ceiling looked familiar but it wasn't the one here in the bedroom. I thought for a moment that Brad Pitt must've whisked me off to some luxurious hotel for the night and I'd have to tell him to get a life. I don't expect he'd argue after trying to get my pants off. I mean, they'd hardly slip easily over my hips, like Geena Davis's in *Thelma and Louise*. I'd probably have to turn onto my stomach so he could try and yank them down over my botty. He'd probably need a slug of whisky at the mere sight of it, let alone anything else.

Talking of large cracks, when I could focus I spotted one in the Artex and realised I must've passed out on the sofa in the living room. Mog jumped onto my chest miaowing to be fed. It was nearly nine o'clock. I was surprised to find a half-eaten pizza in a box on the floor (it's not like me to leave any) with an empty bottle of Chardonnay beside it. Blimey! I felt like Roy Milland in *The Lost Weekend*. I'll be getting the DTs before long if I don't stop all this boozing.

The buzzing started again. I realised my phone was under the cushion beneath my head. I pressed the answer button and a cheery voice asked if I was up for a temporary stint covering reception at a company called Everard's from the following Monday. I was about to say no but thought better of it. I didn't want to start dipping into my redundancy money to pay bills, so I said yes. I felt like shit but would have recovered by then, I reckoned. There was a chance it could be a "temp to perm" arrangement as the current receptionist was leaving in a few weeks' time. Then they broke the news that they wanted me to go right away for a handover as someone had let them down. Aaaaggghhh!

It was too late to backtrack. I staggered into the bathroom half dead. What a sight! Smudged eye make-up, hair on end. Conky had been replaced by Edward Scissorhands minus the scissors and plus a couple of stone.

After several painkillers, two rounds of toast and jam and buckets of strong tea, I yanked on my smart navy linen dress. I hadn't worn it for a while. It was a bit tight but I reckoned it would have to do. I haven't got around to updating my wardrobe, not expecting to be hauled back into the workplace just yet. I put some slap on my face and set off in the car, zigzagging up the road.

Everard's make wooden furniture which I thought was hilarious. I got off on the wrong foot when I said so to the manager Mike as we sat in his office having a chat. My nerves were kicking in by then, hence the tired old joke. I realised from the look on Mike's red face that he was sick of hearing it. He looked pissed off and stressed, probably because of having to tolerate someone new, namely me for a week. He explained how they made mantelpieces and shelving along with tables and chairs to order. Pity they didn't make wooden blinds, too – his office was bloody boiling. They transport all their crap around the UK apparently. Blah, blah, blah, he went on. Yeah, yeah, yeah, I got the gist. I would be covering for someone called Moira while she was on holiday. Reception being the first port of call for visitors I would be expected to reflect the company's image. (Bored stiff and thick as a plank, hahaha!) Anyway, he finally finished waffling and I was taken around the factory by Moira herself (ginger hair – natural not dyed, I reckon). She explained that she was leaving in a few weeks' time to work in her husband's haulage business – hence the possible "temp to perm" – and she was grabbing a week's holiday owed. She showed me who did what. I could hardly hear a thing above all the hammering and sawing. I grasped that Mike wasn't to be disturbed unless absolutely necessary or he'd be inclined to blow a fuse. He'd already blown several, if you ask me.

As with Mike's office, the reception area was stifling. My biggest task was to keep awake and I had to get several coffees from the machine during the morning to do so. Moira nipped into Ashford at lunchtime for some last-minute holiday bits. I envied her jetting off on holiday and looked forward to September when I'd be doing so myself. I took my lunch break when she got back. There was nowhere to go apart from the car, which was like a sauna. I've been meaning to get the air conditioning fixed but haven't got around to it. I expect it'll cost a fortune and they're bound to find half a dozen more things wrong with the car. Roy always used to haggle at garages over the price of repairs but I don't know an alternator from a gear stick, so I'd probably be a sitting duck. I'll have to get it sorted if the hot weather keeps up, though.

I wound the window down and closed my eyes. I took some deep breaths and did that relaxation exercise that Alison does at her yoga class, imagining I was in a deep forest lying under a tree. I've always laughed about it but have to admit I did start to unwind.

I reckoned I'd done well to get to the job in spite of the hangover and felt I deserved a pat on the back. Yeah, I'd made the effort and was earning money. Yeah, a big finger up to Donna and Co.

I felt very peaceful. Birds were singing and I imagined I could even feel moss against my face. A woodpecker tapped. I felt completely at one with nature. Then I heard my name being called somewhere in the distance and woke up to find myself lying across the passenger seat. The woodpecker became Moira rapping on the roof. Bloody hell! That stupid navy dress had ridden up, exposing my bum to the world. I sat up and wiped drool from my mouth as I tried to focus. Several blokes stood outside the factory sniggering. They'd probably had a right old ogle at my nether regions.

Mike walked past, clutching a sandwich. He turned and gave me a funny look. God knows what he must have thought. I apologised to Moira for sleeping ten minutes over my lunch break, but she was quite nice about it. She said she didn't blame me having a snooze but then she would say that, wouldn't she? It was a bit late to get another temp who'd remain alert at all times and wore clothes that fitted.

I called in at Bev's on the way home, hoping for some sisterly sympathy but she just laughed her head off when I told her about those blokes ogling me like that. I said I could've sued for sexual harassment or something. She said it was more likely they'd be suing me for putting them off their lunch (thanks a lot, Sis) and could I babysit over the August Bank Holiday by any chance? I said OK. I won't be doing much else, obviously. I burned that useless navy dress in the brazier at the bottom of the garden as soon as I got back here and it's been trousers ever since. Anyone waiting for another episode of *Whose Cheeks Are They Anyway?* would be greatly disappointed.

A rep came in one morning. He was getting on a bit and introduced himself as Barry Southern, even though he was northern, from Sheffield – that was his standard opening gambit, obviously. I noticed he had a nervous tic with his eyebrows shooting up every few seconds. I thought his life must've been full of surprises and they'd somehow set that way. Barry wasn't bad looking apart from the tic – a bit like Sean Bean gone wrong. He said he was from a company called Planks and could he see the factory manager? I told him Mike had asked not to be disturbed and could he leave his card, but of course he wasn't going to take no for an answer. In the end I had to bite the bullet and ring Mike. I hoped he'd gone to lunch and maybe someone else could come and send Barry on his way but no such luck. Mike answered and as expected, I got my head bitten off. Bloody hell! In this day and age, too! That's something else I should sue for. Mike was obviously familiar with Barry from Planks, who he said was as thick as a plank himself and please get rid of him and 'Sorry to shout, love.'

Meanwhile, Barry was piling hardboard samples onto the coffee table and going on about the external plywood being his bestseller. 'Cuts like a dream and it's great for panelling, sheds, roofing, floors and walls,' he said. 'It's especially good for hand as well as electric sawing and just look at that surface finish.'

From Mike's briefing I knew that Everard's made indoor furniture rather than outdoor stuff, but I couldn't get a word in edgeways to tell Barry what he must already have known. He explained that Planks' plywood was waterproof, boil-proof and resistant to splitting, apparently – unlike himself.

It sounded like he was carrying some hidden baggage as well as samples from the way his hands shook. I didn't encourage him to elaborate as I've had enough crap myself, let's bloody face it. Eventually, he accepted that Mike wasn't any more interested today than the last time he'd called. His cheery smile disappeared and his eyebrows shot up and stayed there as he chucked his samples back into the case and stormed out.

I was surprised to see Barry still sitting in his car when I went out to mine at lunchtime. I'd been taking sandwiches to avoid going anywhere near the canteen. He lowered his window when he saw me. I could see his eyes were a bit red, so I asked if he was OK and whether he'd like a coffee from the machine. He said no thanks, but if I fancied a natter, that would be nice. I didn't really, but I felt sorry for him so I said OK and got in the passenger side.

'It's all been a bit too much lately,' he said. 'First my fiancée leaves me, then I get demoted. I used to be in charge of half of Yorkshire until targets weren't being reached and they brought in someone over my head – younger, of course. They offered me this bit of the south-east or nothing. I'm sure they just sent me down here for a laugh. No way am I meeting any kind of target and the boss knows it. He's only looking for an excuse. Tell you the truth, I'm near the end of me rope.'

'Sorry you've had so much bad luck,' I said. 'What happened with the fiancée, if you don't mind me asking?'

'She was carrying on with the bloke next door. I came home early and found them in the shed together. I couldn't believe it. I'd only gone down there for some 3-in-One Oil cos the gate squeaked.'

Blimey! I didn't know what to say so I just said, 'That's awful,' which it was.

'It had been going on for a while, apparently. She was gonna tell me that night but I'd got home early. I felt sick, I can tell yer. I begged her to think again. I'm a fool, I know, but I'd have forgiven her everything if she'd only change her mind.'

I knew the feeling.

'She gave me the ring back, packed her bags and went next door. She's been there ever since. That was a couple of months ago now. I ought to have gone round there and decked him, but what was the point? He's got the house on the market now. So, they'll be off soon. I'll probably never see her again…'

'I'm really sorry.'

I hoped he wasn't going to start crying again.

'She said I was too intense. Too full on. That's why my first wife left me, she reckoned, but how else can you be if you love someone?'

Search me, I thought. He took a little box from his pocket and took out the sapphire ring inside.

'Cost me a fortune, but I'd have given her anything she wanted to tell you the truth.'

He held it up to the light. I told him it was beautiful.

'You can try it on if you like,' he said.

'Oh, no…'

'Go on, just try it on your finger.'

I did, just to please him, but quickly took it off again. As he took it back he dropped it accidentally and looked down to his feet in search of it. I could see it behind his shoe, so I stretched across him and managed to get it. Just as I was straightening up, Mike passed by the window clutching a baguette. I nodded and smiled but he just stared at me and walked on.

I wished Barry well. It was comforting to know that I wasn't the only one who had been through the mill. I was going to suggest he look me up if he was in the area but it probably wasn't a good idea.

The rest of the week went quickly. I made a real effort to be pleasant to everyone that phoned or called in but the graduation to "perm" never got mentioned.

Mike had obviously made up his mind about someone who slept on the job displaying her wares and gave lunchtime "extras" in the car park.

●

My next job was at a place which created law exam papers near Canterbury. It sounded monotonous (and was) but I thought I'd better give it a try. It could turn into a contract of several months if it worked out OK. I didn't get off to a great start with Rhonda the receptionist when I parked in one of the directors' bays by mistake. Blimey, what a fuss! I should have known that was the shape of things to come. Rhonda escorted me to the office where I'd be based. Someone – probably an ex-employee – had pinned a large paper circle to the filing cabinet, above which was a notice saying "Bang Head Here".

Geraldine, the manager of the department, was probably in her forties. She spoke with a slight lisp and had a short "pageboy" hairstyle which, apart from being years out of date, looked as though it had been cut around a pudding bowl. She had beady little eyes and reminded me of a kid at school who wore round glasses and never took off her mac. She also reminded me of an animal but I couldn't think which one. She probably had the same idea about me as I towered over her. After greeting me with a limp handshake (why bother?) she explained that the job was making amendments to examination questions. These went back and forth between the proofreaders and the typist – namely me – until the completed papers finally got printed.

I made a start on the first batch of papers. From the rare occasions I'd been paying attention at the law firm I recognised some of the legal terminology at least. This was a bonus as I'd forgotten my reading glasses and had to get very close to the screen and squint all that first day. Meanwhile, when she wasn't whispering into her phone (how rude is that?), Geraldine patrolled up and down behind me overseeing my work, or trying to. I would swivel the chair slightly to whichever side she was standing on so that she couldn't see the screen – a bonus of having a broad back.

I wasn't surprised when one of the girls told me in the kitchen that Geraldine wasn't a popular member of staff. No one liked her – apart from her friend Erika, who looked like a prison warder (male) – and there'd been quite a turnover of people in my role over the last few months. I didn't want to get drawn into petty office politics, so I just said, 'Really?' and concentrated on the more important matter of my lunch.

Back in the office I tried to put the police presence out of my mind and just get on with it. The time passed quickly enough but the work was precise and very detailed. By the end of each day my eyes were more crossed than Roy's before the op. I got awful headaches and was popping paracetamol like sweets.

I got a reprieve from my "stalker" one afternoon

when Geraldine went to a meeting. I'd nearly finished the first set of papers so I took a few minutes out to decide which animal she reminded me of. Eventually, I came up with a baboon. I know Alison would say it was childish but I looked at some baboons on the Internet and found definite similarities between Geraldine and the Hamadryas breed. It had weird hair around its face for a start and really small eyes.

The exam question I had on the screen at the time was "*In what scenario would it be necessary to describe the defendant's appearance?*" I typed in the answer box "*It is necessary to describe the defendant, Geraldine's, appearance because she is an overbearing, conceited baboon. She looks like one, acts like one and if you were to get really close, which I avoid doing, she probably smells like one. Her bottom is probably bright pink just like a baboon's. God knows how anyone would fancy her in a million years...*"

I was just about to add "*Like the Hamadryas, Geraldine can move noiselessly through the undergrowth...*" when suddenly she proved this to be true and was back in the room! Bloody hell!

'Have you finished those papers?' she asked while I quickly tried to shrink the page down, swivelling to and fro like mad, trying to gauge which shoulder she was about to peer over. It was a bloody good job that someone came in to ask her a question just then and I could delete my handiwork. Bloomin' close shave, though.

A couple of days later, Geraldine suggested a trip to the printers in Dover so I could see how the exam papers were printed and put together. I said OK. At least it meant a day out of the office without her breathing down my neck.

Things went askew from the start when I overslept. I'd set the bloody alarm for 6p.m. instead of 6a.m. so had to go like the clappers. I took a wrong turn somewhere, got lost and then hit a load of traffic. (I really need to invest in a satnav as well as aircon.) I'd meant to pick up a sandwich but I was already late. By the time I got there the bloke who was meant to show me around had gone out. The receptionist said Geraldine and her colleagues were working through a buffet lunch if I wanted to join them. I hadn't bargained on Geraldine being there. I guess she just wanted to surprise me. I thought I'd better show my face. Besides, I was starving and a working lunch meant food. Who knew? Maybe the baboon was a different animal away from the office and would ask me to pull up a seat and tuck in.

I made my way down the corridor towards a glass-panelled office. In the middle of the table were platters of sandwiches. I could see Geraldine giving a presentation to members of staff as they ate. Several heads turned to look at me, including Geraldine's who was obviously the same animal both in and out of the office because she ignored me altogether and carried on gibbering. I hovered there for a minute, not knowing quite what to do. Then I knew exactly. I turned around and walked out. I was buggered if I was going to be made a monkey of by a baboon. She could stick her sodding exam papers right up her pink bottom, set them alight and fire herself out of a cannon for all I cared.

I would've come straight home then, but remembered I'd left my new red blazer in the office. Bloody hell! When I got back there, the prison warder was on patrol. Obviously primed by the baboon she asked me what I thought I was doing coming back so early without having the printing works tour – like I was about five? OK, Alison says I act like it sometimes but blimey! I couldn't even be bothered to answer. I grabbed my blazer, chucked her the keys to the filing cabinet (without banging my head or hers on it although I was tempted) and walked out.

I was a few yards from reception when an alarm went off. I thought it might be to alert HR that I was trying to escape but it turned out to be the fire drill. People were coming out of their offices smiling as they joined me on the way to the exit. I smiled back but for a different reason. I wasn't going back in.

Rhonda was counting heads as everyone passed reception, telling them to go and stand beneath a large oak tree – the designated assembly point should the place ever suddenly burst into flames.

I made a detour towards the car with Rhonda shouting behind me that I was going the wrong way. I got in, revved up and screeched off, narrowly missing her as she frantically tried to wave me down. To infinity and beyond! Ha ha! Bloody good riddance!

The London Experience

A reference letter arrived signed by Donna on behalf of the management, acknowledging my ten years' loyal service and wishing me luck in the future. Not the most glowing reference but better than nothing, I suppose. Alison suggested I try working further afield – London maybe, less than an hour away by train. I told her I couldn't see myself going up there every day but I emailed my CV to a couple of agencies in any case. I was amazed when one of them replied suggesting I should call in the next time I was in town. They were based near Liverpool Street Station and easy enough to get to from St Pancras.

Alison said I should make an appointment as soon as possible, which got me all of a dither. She recommended I do a spelling test online beforehand, obviously with "skellington" in mind. I told her that was a one-off but she said just to be on the safe side.

Questions popped up on the screen such as:

"The train was stationery – correct or incorrect?"

(Stationary, obviously – you'd have to be really thick not to know that.)

"Mrs Smith was the school principle" – correct or incorrect?"

(That, too.)

"The populis revolted – correct or incorrect?"

I thought, eh? Where would you ever need to use that word apart from in ancient Rome? I pressed "correct" but it turned out to be "populace". That one really caught me on the hop, I must say. I did a speed test too, which wasn't great, thanks to the few months I'd spent with that snail Barnett, but I managed not to make any mistakes at least. This morning I braved the windy weather and set off for London.

I was a bit stewed up on the train wondering what the hell I was doing till I reminded myself that the agency had been impressed enough by my CV to want to see me. Once there, I filled out a form for Mel the consultant who wasn't exactly twelve but not much more. She and her colleagues were immaculately dressed and very self-assured. I thought of myself at their age – talk about a contrast. My self-esteem was always minus zero back then. I would laugh at myself to make up for it. As for my dress sense, that hasn't improved much either. When Mel reached into a cupboard for something, its mirrored door swung open and for a moment I thought a tramp had come in off the street until I realised it was me. My black moccasins, purchased only a month ago, were already scuffed and my red blazer looked way too bright. My hair had gone full on bouffant in the wind and I hadn't so much as a comb with me. Forget about being a PA; I reckoned I could've got a job outside Buckingham Palace, own headgear supplied.

Mel went through my CV. Three jobs of long duration looked good on paper at least. The first at the stationery company was a long time ago, before Mel was born. I told her I'd done the post and worked in the copying room. My reason for leaving was due to the arrival of email. No one wrote letters any more. The firm had gone bust.

'It's hard to imagine life without email!' said Mel, fascinated. I laughed. I suppose it must've seemed like when dinosaurs ruled the earth to her. I went on to explain how I'd graduated into the legal field with my next job, working for a law firm for several years before they went into liquidation.

'Was it me?' I joked but Mel didn't respond. Instead, she asked me to describe my job at the legal practice. I told her I'd been "float" and stood in for people when they were away or off sick. Mel said yes, she knew what float meant, which was a bit bloomin' cheeky, I thought. I explained how I'd manned the reception as well. I thought afterwards what a silly word "manned" is to use in that context – as if working a switchboard and greeting visitors had required intense physical labour usually done by half a dozen men. I'd got "manned" from some out-of-date CV templates on the Internet, along with words like "tact and diplomacy" and "poised"

– poised for what? Poised on one leg like a chicken in case the boss wants a cup of tea? What about "providing backup"? That's another one. *"Oh, the silly sod can't find his meeting papers. I'd better call for backup..."* like the cops on telly.

It made me realise what a boring career I'd chosen, although really it chose me if truth be told. I'd taken that first job in my teens until I found something more interesting to do but somehow never had. I should have studied harder and gone on to become a professional of some sort (although professional what, I don't know – professional twit maybe). All those years of service since leaving school while I was deciding what to do with myself hadn't gone to waste exactly, but Alison had bigged up my CV beyond belief. According to her, my float role had given me "a wealth of experience and I had much to offer in a more prestigious environment".

From this, Mel had probably expected a polished high-achiever looking to move on in her already glittering career. There was also the minor detail of my age. Alison had left it off of the CV, saying it was discriminatory nowadays, but of course it would rear its fifty-year-old head eventually.

Mel went on about the firms she dealt with having high expectations of their employees. Some offered training for staff, enabling them to become strong team members in order to attain their goals. (I thought I was there to get a job as a personal assistant not a reserve for

Queens Park Rangers.) She explained that her clients in the legal field dealt with major multinationals, financial institutions, private businesses and wealthy individuals. They sounded swish and high-flying, a long way from that old stick, Hardcastle.

She said that short-term contracts were the best way of learning about a company's culture and it was just a pity there weren't any of these available at the moment. Obviously, there weren't any that I'd be suitable for. Basically, I'd wasted my time and rail fare in finding out what I should have known already – I'm over the hill.

Having started the interview, pointless as it was, Mel probably thought she might as well see it through and ran down a list of questions like was I good at working as part of a team?

(No, I hate having to work with other people; office politics get on my wick…)

I said yes, of course, and that I was a good mixer which reminded me to pick up a bottle of lemonade on the way home to go with a few whiskies later.

Then she asked what did I feel I could bring to my next job?

(A few sandwiches if there's no canteen, my own broom if it was road-sweeping, and don't forget my busby for Buck House…)

I said "a positive attitude", of course.

How were my communication skills?

Wot?

I told her I was good at keeping up to speed. *(I'd done eighty on the motorway the other day.)* I interacted well with others and was always ready to go the extra mile to help a colleague out. *(Go and ask someone else, I'm busy...)*

Where did I see myself in five years' time?

(Holloway.)

Of course I answered, 'In a progressive role where my experience will be put to good use,' wondering if I'd make the next train home which left in half an hour.

We touched on my education. I told her I'd done RSA Typing Stage Three and Pitmans shorthand at 100 words per minute. All old hat now, no doubt. Her top-end clients probably wanted degrees. She asked about exams and had I done any A-levels? I said no, only Os. I'd done O level English, History and of course, French. My certificate was lost years ago, but I just told her I got Grade One in everything and of course I'd passed my Eleven Plus.

'It was an exam that decided whether you went to the grammar school or secondary modern,' I explained.

'Yes, they still have it now,' Mel assured me.

My confidence was slowly deflating Conky-style. I reminded myself that I'd actually made it to the grammar school, which was quite a turn up at the time. Dad was very proud but Mum said she couldn't believe I'd managed it and had I been cribbing off someone else? She said I stood a good chance of making something of my life after all. I might've done if I hadn't been so busy staring out of the window or giggling with my friends and fulfilling my role in light entertainment.

Mel said she would be in touch if anything came in. I took that to mean in the tea-lady line until I realised that, like me, they're almost extinct.

I sloped out. The wind and rain hit me full in the face, beating me up. Back in Ashford I treated myself to the usual comfort food – a large cod and chips. I got the expected dressing down from Alison over a glass of wine this evening.

'Gloria, you had every chance of carrying it off today had you for once in your life, just believed in yourself,' she said. 'Instead, you let yourself be intimidated by someone half your age. Something you hoped to avoid from the outset.'

'It's your fault for blowing my CV up out of all proportion,' I told her.

'There's no point in hiding your light under a bushel.'

'Yes but it was way over the top. That girl could see straight through me and obviously thought I was a played-out old bag the minute I walked in.'

'Gloria, for God's sake! You're fifty years old, as you keep reminding me. Well, be proud of being fifty and all the experience that goes with it! OK, you've had a few knock-backs, but so bloody what? It's time to stop making excuses for yourself. Think positive for once.'

I knew she was right, but I didn't know where all this confidence was supposed to come from. I felt like booing but was determined not to. As usual, she guessed when

I started sniffing and pushed a box of tissues along the table towards me with her toe.

'Look, I've been thinking. What about renting out the spare room?'

'Eh?' I said, blowing my nose.

'The landlord needn't know and hey, you might get a tall dark stranger turning up.'

I said no, that was way too scary, then I thought about it and said yes, why not? I had nothing to lose.

The Landlady

I was terrified at the prospect, but yeah, taking a lodger might be the way to go. I plucked up courage and put a card in Raj's window yesterday advertising the spare room for rent. I reminded myself I needn't take anyone if I didn't like the look of them. I went to the DIY store this morning and picked up some stuff to give the hallway a facelift in case a suitable lodger materialises. I painted over the areas Roy had touched during his visit, making it a totally Roy-free zone. I checked with the agency that the landlord had no objection to having the hall decorated for nothing. They said there was no problem. He probably doesn't care what I do as long as he gets his rent every month. I was halfway through painting the ceiling when Tracey turned up with Sinbad in the buggy.

'Thought I'd have a look at your new place,' she said. It was good to see her. I thought she might've taken her dad's side and written me off, but she said she was surprised I'd put up with him as long as I did. I asked if she'd been to see him at Smeeth.

'I ain't speaking to 'im, am I?' she replied. 'He hates 'Lijah for a start. We wouldn't fit into his posh new life. It's like he's turned his back on us. Lije says he'd like to get him in a half nelson until he begs for mercy.'

Sinbad was asleep (thank God) so Tracey and I had a good chat while she stood smoking cigarettes out of the back door. Elijah, who'd been to his wrestling club, turned up an hour or so later, moving around the place like a trapped bull, opening drawers and nosing in cupboards. I tried to imagine facing him in the wrestling ring – it must be horrific. He looked even bigger in the small kitchen I've got here as he demonstrated how he could pick Tracey up with one arm. When he spotted the broken phone table in the understairs cupboard he asked if he could take it off my hands. He reckoned even though its legs were bust, its copper feet were worth something. I haven't got around to dumping it so was only too pleased to let him have it.

Sinbad woke up then and started yelling like an air-raid siren, so they left. It was great to see them and to know they're on my side. I can't believe Roy would cut his own daughter and grandson out of his life. He can't see beyond the pug, that's the trouble. He's in a mid-life crisis obviously, trying to keep hold of what he thinks he needs at any price. Well, good luck to him. More and more I realise, he's one useless git and I reckon it won't be long before the pug herself sniffs out the truth. Then there's Tracey, stuck with a baby at nineteen when she should be out enjoying herself – but of course Sinbad will grow up. When he's twenty, Tracey will be forty and still young. She'll be a grandmother one day. Sinbad will visit with his kids. They'll remember her birthday and at Christmas. How can I criticise Tracey when here I am at fifty with nothing to show for it? Bearing in mind what Alison said about thinking positive and believing in myself, it's not easy to shake off the past. I'm still dragging all that baggage around with me like Robert De Niro in *The Mission*. How could I have done things any differently?

Like Barry said, if you love someone you look after them and that's what I did with Roy. All I want in a man is a friend – someone to come home to and who cares about me – I mean really cares. Alison always says she doesn't need a man in her life (although she wouldn't say no to that tosser Joe in Majorca, I reckon) but I do. I'm bloomin' lonely and just want to share my life with someone who won't let me down. Is that too much to ask? Yes, obviously. How do you meet anyone these days, anyway? In Auntie Kit's day at the Corn Exchange, men asked girls to dance. You said yes if you liked the look of them. Then a date might be set up and things went from there. Whenever a slow dance came on at the discos I went to in the eighties, I'd head to the toilets, rather than hang about waiting for an awkward shuffle with someone several inches shorter than me.

Mum and Dad met at a whist drive – totally rocking (not). No dancing involved. Mum had only gone along with a friend to make up the numbers. They hadn't been very well suited on looking back. Dad wasn't exciting enough for Mum. George was hardly George Clooney (more like George Loony, actually) but he'd impressed her with his dinner suit and rendition of "That's Amore". He'd also showered her with compliments and full-on attention, which she'd lapped up. If I hadn't made a move on Roy that night in the County bar, nothing would've happened. He would certainly never have approached me, that's for sure. He hadn't long lost his mum. I suppose I was a kind of replacement.

I was thinking about all of this as I finished painting the hallway. I tidied up and was just sitting down to a pizza (Hawaiian) when a bloke called about the room! I couldn't believe it! I managed to keep my voice calm, as if I let out rooms all the time. His name was Phil and he said sorry it was late but was there any way he could pop round and have a quick look? I assumed he was talking about the room but you never know. I said OK, then got Alison to come over.

I reckoned Phil was about thirty-five, not tall but he does have dark hair. His face is roundish and his nose is a bit squashed at the end, like it's pressing against something invisible – a window maybe, which made me worry that he might be a peeping Tom at least. I just had to trust my instincts as to how he came across. Alison did most of the talking anyway.

Phil explained that he was born in Ashford and lived here until he met his wife, Gwynnie (now ex) who was from Port Talbot. They lived there for five years until they decided to call it a day. He works in London now in the HR department of a law firm in Holborn and wants to move back here and commute. He's only looking for somewhere short term till he finds a house. He said the couple of rentals he'd seen in the area asked for a six-month arrangement which he didn't want to commit to. He'd called in to Raj's for the local paper and seen my card in the window.

'What luck!' said Alison. 'I think this is meant to be!'

She shook hands with Phil like it was a done deal and then hurried off to a dinner date with friends. I was left standing there with him in the kitchen, which was a bit embarrassing as I couldn't think of anything to say. He asked me what I did and I told him I'd also worked for a legal firm until I was let go recently. He sympathised and said he'd had to let a few go in Port Talbot himself. I suppose it was nerves but I wanted to laugh out loud as I imagined him farting his way around Port Talbot. He said it must be awful to be on the receiving end which only made it worse. Hahaha! I don't know how I kept a straight face. Anyway, he said he liked the room. I waited for the "but" to follow, meaning the prospect of sharing a house with me wasn't too appealing. No "but" came, though.

I couldn't believe it when he said he was happy to pay the £650 per month and would transfer the first payment plus the deposit to my bank immediately! He said he was very house-trained and would be out a lot of the time, either at work or checking properties. He asked if it was OK to move in next Saturday so I said yes. I noticed his cologne still lingered after he left – a sort of lemony smell. I texted Alison with the news. She texted back *Fantastic!* and that it would probably be strange having a man around again. I reminded her I'd had Roy for ten years. She replied *No, a man.*

●

Phil moved in yesterday. I've been preparing for it all week – scrubbing and dusting and cleaning windows, or at least the one in the kitchen which always gets spattered from the sink. I hate cleaning that window – the sink gets me right in the stomach. I gave a few finishing touches to the spare room, including a new duvet set and a bedside rug. I bought three new beige towels – small, medium and large and put them on the bed. I got a unisex shower gel and some plain soap.

Phil turned up around three o'clock. He didn't have much stuff as most of it's in storage in Port Talbot. He unpacked his case and had a cup of tea. He was quite chatty and any reservations I'd had about him quickly disappeared. Then he took off to meet some old friends in town. I'd forgotten to get another key cut for the front door, so I left mine under the plant pot for him. I also showed him the trick with the lock, which unlike Roy he seemed to grasp right away. He asked if I was I going out. I said no – I was staying in with a movie and a glass of wine. (As if I ever do anything else.) He looked nice when he came downstairs in a crisp white shirt which showed off his dark hair. He said he'd try not to wake me when he came in. I went all red at the thought of him waking me in any circumstances and told myself to get a grip.

After he'd gone I had a butcher's at his room. His suitcase was on top of the wardrobe and he'd hung up a couple of suits and some shirts inside. There were some trainers and two pairs of leather shoes in black and tan. His toilet bag was on the dressing table containing the lemony cologne which I tried on my finger. There were silk ties in the top drawer all neatly coiled. His briefcase was on the floor beside the bed. In the bathroom I noticed he'd used the small towel. It was on the radiator slightly damp and he'd also used the new soap.

I heated up some pasta for dinner and watched a film. I couldn't really concentrate for wondering what time Phil would come back. I was woken up just after midnight by the sound of the front door closing. I wondered what the hell was going on until I remembered I had a lodger. I'd had a horrible dream about being chased by a giant suitcase. Everywhere I went, it would loom up in front of me blocking out the light. I heard Phil turn on the kitchen tap and then come upstairs. He went in the bathroom to pee which sounded like thunder. There was a bit of splashing and cleaning of teeth before he went into his room.

●

I ate my cereal while Phil went out jogging this morning. I didn't want him to see me stuffing my face. He said he jogs every day and Sundays are no exception. He showered when he came in, using the large towel, I reckoned. When he came down his hair was still a bit damp and he looked quite nice in jeans and a pale blue shirt. I couldn't help wondering what he wears in bed. Is he a jim-jam man? I didn't see any during my inspection. Maybe he's a T-shirt and boxers type? Maybe just the boxers? Maybe nothing at all. Oo-er!

He said he'd had a curry in town with some old mates last night and he hoped he hadn't disturbed me and how was my film? I couldn't remember what I'd watched – something about murder in the swamps in the Deep South. I tried to explain what happened in it but Phil's eyes started to glaze over. He's obviously got me down as some sort of sad mollusc. He asked if I wanted anything from Raj's as he was going for the paper. I said no and did he fancy something hot? I meant to say a cooked breakfast and went red again. God knows what he must think of me, silly big bitch. Anyway, he said yes please, if it wasn't too much trouble so I did sausage, egg and bacon.

By the time Phil got back the kitchen was full of steam. I tried to open the window behind the sink, but it was stuck as usual so he stretched across me smelling all lemony and opened it easy as pie. He said all it needed was a good yank upwards. I said, 'oo-er!' and felt really stupid when he didn't laugh. To make things worse I told him the window in my bedroom was stuck as well. I don't know what possessed me. It sounded like an invitation – a line from a *Carry On* film. *Carry On Landlady,* maybe. I blushed again and quickly turned the sausages under the grill.

Phil said a couple of new windows wouldn't be too expensive and would add value to the house. I said yeah, probably. I wasn't going to confess to only renting the place. I asked him what Port Talbot was like. Then I regretted bringing the subject up in case he was sensitive about his divorce but he volunteered the information, saying that he and Gwynnie had found they wanted different things. Their decision to split had been mutual. He offered to wash up which I thought was very polite, but I said no and thanks anyway. He went out to meet friends again. After he left I had another peep in his room which was still neat and tidy. I was right about the big towel as it was damp and hanging over the bathroom radiator. His wet footprints were on the bathmat. I fitted my own feet into them to compare sizes. As expected, there wasn't much difference.

●

Phil's been here a month now. He certainly meant what he said about not being around a great deal. He's always gone by six-thirty in the morning during the week after his jog. He's quite stocky and I reckon it wouldn't take much for him to become a bit of a chunkster if he let himself go. At weekends he jogs at seven. He was on the phone after he got back this morning, arranging to see friends for the usual Saturday get-together. I looked over the bannister to where he was standing and could see some chest hair poking out of the top of his T-shirt – just a sprinkling. I'd gone right off hairy chests after I went out with that Bob bloke just before I met Roy. He looked like he was wearing a gorilla suit when he undressed and got really annoyed when I asked where the zip was. I only meant it as a joke, but it certainly put the kybosh on things. Some people are so sensitive!

While Phil planned his day I caught sight of myself in the bathroom mirror and decided I need to pay more attention to my appearance in the mornings. I ought to get up earlier and make myself presentable. Slobbing about in a dressing gown looking like Mrs Rochester in *Jane Eyre* is just not on.

After Phil had gone I did a bit of a tidy-up and put fresh towels on his bed. I wondered if I should do his washing as the weather was fine and his laundry basket was quite full. Second thoughts, he isn't paying me to wash his smalls or mediums or, God forbid, larges and he might be a bit embarrassed at me handling his Calvin Kleins. I've told him he can put a wash on whenever he likes though. He's been doing it on Sundays at an off-peak time to save me money. How disciplined he is! Talking of discipline, I wondered if Roy really goes to the gym nowadays like he said he does. I had to laugh thinking of him on the running machine gasping for breath – his Emu legs going nineteen to the dozen and falling arse-over-head off of it. Hahaha!

●

Phil brought in a curry this evening after looking at a couple of houses. We chatted about his work in HR. I told him of my temping experiences and how I daren't put my age on my CV. Of course this prompted him to enquire as to the actual number (if I didn't mind him asking). I did, but there was no going back then so I had to confess to the half century. He said I didn't look it but then he would say that, wouldn't he? Turns out he's forty-one. I said he didn't look it either. On the positive side, he said age meant experience. I felt like saying yeah, in being a loser in my case, but I didn't.

After the curry, Phil had to do some paperwork so I left him to it and went in the lounge to watch *The Graduate*. I've seen it loads of times but always find the affair between Benjamin and the older woman Mrs Robinson quite thrilling. Mrs Robinson now seems a lot younger than me, which is rather worrying though. I admire her confidence in seducing Benjamin. It reminds me of the night I invited Roy to come upstairs and wrap his skinny legs around me. That was a bit of a gamble and no mistake. I wondered what Phil would do if I put on a pair of black fishnet stockings, went down to the kitchen and flashed a leg at him across the table – always assuming I could get it up that high of course.

I thought perhaps I could compromise by leaning on a chair, hitching up my skirt and pouting at him in a tantalising way. Probably not a good idea after a chicken shashlik. I thought he might come into the living room later for a nightcap to round off the evening, but he got a call from a mate suggesting a late drink in town. Off he went and I turned upstairs to bed. *Hello, darkness, my old friend…*

The Babysitter

Having agreed to babysit Kim, Nessa and Kevin over the Bank Holiday weekend, I didn't really feel like moving into Bev's for three nights. I know it's silly but I've got used to having the occasional chat with Phil. He's usually around more at the weekends, even though they involve house-hunting and meeting up with his mates.

Bev's was a madhouse as usual when I arrived. She was putting last-minute bits and pieces into a suitcase and bellowing to Kim and Nessa to stop thumping around upstairs. Kevin was toddling around putting toys into the case. I hoped there wouldn't be uproar when he realised he wasn't going with his mum and dad. They left around ten after warning the kids to behave themselves or they'd get no presents. Luckily, Kevin didn't make a fuss. I was instructed to make sure Matty ate something healthy when he came in later. Apparently, he was getting too fond of biking round to the Chinese with his mates for chips in curry sauce. It was still only Friday.

I tried not to think about the bleak weekend stretching ahead and got stuck into the washing up, only to be stuck in the bum cheek by Kevin's plastic sword. It was really sore and caused a massive bruise on my blubber.

Kim and Nessa carried on thumping about in their room all afternoon. I found them playing a game of Helicopter Rescue on their bunk beds. Kim, on top, was trying to hoist Nessa up from "the sea" with a dressing-gown sash tied around her middle. I reminded them that they were six and eight and not babies – not that babies played Helicopter Rescue but they knew what I meant. We watched telly after tea and later on Kevin fell asleep on the sofa so I carried him upstairs to bed around seven thirty. The girls were still messing about. It was too much of a novelty having Auntie around. Matty came in around nine o'clock and threatened the pair of them with a "nutting" if they didn't do as they were told. Big brother had spoken and it was soon quiet up there. Sticking to Bev's instructions, I'd saved Matty some quiche and salad but he'd brought in chips and curry sauce. I knew I should've laid down the law but joined him in a chip butty instead.

On Saturday I took the girls and Kevin to the funfair at Dymchurch. I'd promised to wake Matty for his paper round but failed miserably. Luckily, he had set his alarm – a cock crowing – for 6a.m. I'd thought it was coming from a distant farm and went back to sleep.

It was a long drive to Dymchurch, but as always we had fun when we got there. Kim took Kevin on the little roundabout while I went on the ghost train with Nessa. She said it was a bit "pants". I agreed, but shrieked my head off all the way through just the same. When the usual high-pitched siren signalled the end of the ride, I tried to hide my disappointment. After a go on the bumper cars we did the water ride and all got wet. My glasses were steamed up and I couldn't see to climb out. The kids laughed their heads off at Auntie groping the air.

Kevin slept all the way home and the girls sang songs they'd learned at school. It took me back to my own schooldays. Primary school wasn't bad but I remembered being pleased when I left the grammar to embark on an exciting future which didn't actually happen. I can't even blame it on bringing up kids. What sort of mother would I have made when I act like a big kid myself? Alison's right about me being childish. I wonder whether the kids will visit their daft old bat of an auntie in her nursing home when I'm in my dotage. Probably not.

When we got home the kids wanted "Hedgehog" for tea, which meant making a huge mound of mashed spud and sticking small sausages all over it. They wanted to stay up late so I made popcorn and put on an *Austin Powers* film. I wondered if I'd done the right thing when they roared laughing at words like "shag" and "Fat Bastard".

Matty came in later with a tin of shandy and more curried chips which everyone dipped into. Sprawled across an armchair he said the bloke next door looked just like Fat Bastard and probably ate his own poo as well.

'It's a bit nutty!' he said, which had everyone in hysterics including myself, setting a good example as ever.

Yesterday (Sunday) morning, I found Kevin on the living room sofa watching cartoons. The kitchen door was wedged shut with a lot of movement and giggling coming from the other side. I was dying for a coffee and my patience was wearing thin. When the girls finally opened up I expected to see a hell of a mess everywhere but couldn't believe my eyes. There were rose petals scattered over the table on which was a sandwich of burnt toast piled high with a flattened hard-boiled egg and cherry tomatoes. There was also a mug of instant cappuccino by the side of the plate.

'Well, what do you think, Auntie?' Nessa asked after pushing the sandwich down with a chubby fist. I said it was a meal fit for a queen. Kim said that was good because I was one. I sat down and tried to eat but it was difficult. Not because of the height of the sandwich but due to a big lump in my throat.

I took Kevin and the girls to the swimming pool at Tenterden later on. I was going to take photos of them larking about in the water for their mum and dad before I remembered you can't do that nowadays without raising suspicions of the paedo kind. Kevin didn't want to get out so I had to tempt him with a chocolate bar. They ate the banana rolls I'd packed on the way home.

The car smelled of banana, chlorine and damp kids. I did pizza and salad for tea but no one ate the salad, wanting baked beans instead. Matty said he'd get chips in curry sauce later. Oh well, I tried at least.

●

By the time Bev and Darren got back this afternoon, I was shattered but I'd enjoyed being with the kids. We'd kind of bonded again as always happens when I stay a couple of nights. They all got presents for being good. Kevin's was a plastic dagger. I got a bottle of wine and a lot of thanks. Then the kids went out to play and Matty went off to find his mates. Everything was back to normal. Bev started filling the washing machine so I left her to it and toddled off feeling redundant all over again.

Phil wasn't here when I got back – not that I expected him to be, although it would have been nice. I'd been thinking a lot about him over the weekend – which isn't healthy, I know. Mog's bowl was empty and she scoffed the food I put down in seconds. Alison was supposed to feed her but must have forgotten.

I had a peek in Phil's room and was shocked to find an empty champagne bottle on the floor and a pink thong beside it – charming! How dare he drag women back here as soon as I'm out of the way! Talk about taking advantage! I thought of all those bloody cooked breakfasts I've done for him, not to mention the shower gel and two sets of towels! I went downstairs and had a good old cry.

Alison texted a bit later. Did I fancy some dinner? She'd made shepherd's pie for her parents yesterday and there was loads left. I was about to text back saying the last thing I felt like doing was eating but I went over in any case and took Bev's wine with me. I sat at the table while Alison flitted to and fro with cutlery and stuff. I felt dizzy and a bit sick, but the shepherd's pie smelled good so I thought I'd better try and force some down. I reckoned I'd feel a lot better with a glass of that red wine inside me too, but Alison was boiling the kettle for tea. She said yesterday's lunch with her parents had been a struggle due to an enormous hangover from Saturday night. She'd gone out around town with a few friends apparently and apologised for forgetting to feed the cat.

'Oh, by the way,' she said, 'I saw Phil in Wetherspoons.'

'What?' I said. 'When?'

'Saturday. He was with a few mates on a stag do. They were all wearing thongs.'

'You saw him in Wetherspoons?'

'Yes,' she said. 'It was a stag do.'

'And they were all wearing thongs?'

'Yes, over their trousers. What is this, *Marple*?'

A few moments went by while this sunk in. Alison put two mugs of tea on the table and sat down.

'What's up?' she said, homing in on my face. 'You look weird.'

'Oh, nothing… nothing,' I said. 'That explains it.'

'Explains what?'

I told her how I'd found the pink thong in Phil's room, along with an empty bottle of champagne and tried to pass it off with a laugh.

'And you put two and two together and came up with five,' she said. 'Oh, Gloria, I hope you're not…'

'Not what?' I said, eyes wide.

'You know, not getting too… attached to Phil.'

'What?' I said. 'Don't be stupid! He's just a nice bloke, that's all. What he gets up to is his business. He can come and go as he likes. I just found the thong and thought it was a bit unusual, that's all. I mean, if he'd brought some slapper back while I was away, which as it turns out he didn't, I think I'd have a right to get a bit annoyed about it, don't you?'

'From what I've seen of Phil I don't think he would do that, Gloria. Don't forget, I'm a pretty good judge of character where men are concerned. How's his house-hunting coming along anyway?'

'Oh, he hasn't found anything yet,' I assured her.

'He will though, won't he?'

'I expect so, but there's no point in rushing things, is there? He seems quite happy at the moment.'

'As long as you keep things in perspective.'

I said, 'What's that supposed to mean?'

'You need to stop daydreaming about things you can't have and get a life, Gloria.'

'I'm not!' I assured her. 'You've really got the wrong end of the stick.'

The trouble is Alison can always see right through me. My chin started to wobble. It also had some mash on it which she pointed out and passed me some kitchen roll.

'Sorry, Gloria,' she went on. 'But I'm being cruel to be kind. I don't want you to get hurt again. Also, you need to stop hitting the bottle every time something goes wrong.'

I dabbed my eyes and said that was bloody rich coming from someone who'd been half-dead with a hangover the previous day.

'Yes,' she said, 'but I'm a social drinker. I don't use alcohol as a prop the way you do. I just have a glass of wine with dinner and that's it. I can do without it.'

I told her drink was just a comfort at the moment, like chocolate.

'If you want to cut down, I can help. We'll do it together. What do you think?'

'OK,' I said, trying to sound enthusiastic. 'If you like.'

We lifted our mugs and chinked.

'Here's to new things,' said Alison.

'New thongs you mean…'

She laughed and choked and ran to the sink to spit out the tea.

'I was thinking I might get myself one for the holiday,' I told her.

'Would that be a thong for Europe?' she asked when she could speak.

'The size of Europe probably,' I said. 'By the way…'

'What?'

'A drop of red would really go down well with this pie…'

'I'll get the glasses,' said Alison.

Holiday

I dropped Mog off at the cattery in Wye this morning. I couldn't expect Phil to feed her while I'm away. It looks as if he may have found a house he likes with no "chain" and could move out any day. I'm trying not to think about that. This holiday has probably come at the right time, all things considered.

Bloody roadworks were blocking the lane outside Wye, so there was a queue a mile long. Mog knew something was up – her carry-case usually means the vets and she miaowed all the way there. She hissed at the cattery owner when she looked inside the case, which wasn't a very good start. I apologised for her being a bit nervy and said I had to dash as I was already late. I'd forgotten Mog's food and was told some would have to be bought and added to the bill (already huge).

Alison complained about leaving late for the airport, of course. OK, we were a little behind but what was the point in being there two hours ahead when we'd already checked in online? As luck would bloody well have it there'd been an accident causing a tailback near Clacket Lane Services. Naturally, Alison blamed me for that, saying if only we'd left earlier we'd have missed it. Yeah, how about her driving us to the airport and leaving her car there for a week instead of mine?

I realised that due to rushing I'd forgotten to change into my soft leather loafers, which were by the front door. Instead, I had on a pair of canvas deck shoes. Alison had warned me off them in the shop, saying canvas always made your feet hot. I was having none of it, of course. I thought they looked great and they were fine in cool weather, actually. I found out the hard way that at the slightest hint of heat they'd fry my feet like a couple of saveloys. The heat was building up in the car and I could feel them slowly starting to sizzle.

'Can't you switch the air conditioning on?' said Alison. I broke the news that it wasn't working and told her to open a window, which she did.

'I can't believe it!' she moaned with her hair blowing all over the place. 'How can you have no air con?'

I kept schtum when really I felt like slipping one of my canvas killers off and clobbering her with it.

I haven't been abroad since I went with Roy to Tenerife and that was a while ago. I'd forgotten the drill at the airport. My keys were in the front pocket of my trousers as usual and set the alarm off going through security. Alison had gone on ahead. When she looked back and saw me being frisked she rolled her eyes in despair. Once it was established that I wasn't carrying anything lethal,

I was allowed through. Alison left me with the bags while she went off to buy perfume. By bags, I mean her neat designer number and my floral cheapie, which was stuffed to the gunnels and all out of shape.

I was pleased to see that I wasn't the only one who'd set the alarm screeching. A cool-looking bloke in a linen suit, who I thought resembled Bill Nighy, had set it off too and for the same reason – keys in his pocket. He got frisked and wasn't too happy when they put that wand thing between his legs.

'Bloody hell! Is nothing sacred?' he said. 'And I'll have that back if you don't mind!'

He grabbed his camera after the security bloke had checked inside its case and was all fingers and thumbs as he did up his belt.

'I had the same trouble,' I said sympathetically as he passed by.

'Sorry?' he said crossly.

'Keys in the front pocket.'

He didn't smile back, just looked at me like I was a yeti who'd somehow managed to sneak through on all fours. His hair was quite floppy, I noticed, and a sort of sandy colour. He pushed it away from his face in irritation as he walked off. Blimey, what a misery!

We were right up front in the priority queue when the female attendant behind the desk told me to check the size of my bag in the metal frame provided. It had to fit the exact same dimensions – something I hadn't thought about at the time of purchase. It was pretty obvious even before I started shoving the bag into the frame that it wasn't going to fit. I don't know why but I kept trying, hoping that by some Harry Potter magic it might dwindle down to the correct size. Of course it got well and truly stuck and I couldn't shift it either way. I pulled hard which resulted in both the case and the frame leaving the floor a few inches. By this time people were going through to the plane, some I noticed with cases at least as big as mine by the way. Alison was livid, especially when I suggested she take some of my stuff in her own bag when we got mine out, which didn't look like it was going to be any time soon.

'I've no room for your stuff,' she said through gritted teeth. 'Why did you pack so much cack?'

Just then "Bill" strode up.

'Can I make a suggestion?' he asked. 'If we turn the whole thing over on its side. I'll hold the bottom while you pull it out. That way, we might get on the plane before midnight.'

I did as he said and a few seconds later my case was released on bail. As if to celebrate its newly found freedom, its flimsy lock gave way and my stuff spilled out onto the floor.

'For God's sake!' yelled Alison.

Bill asked where we were staying. I told him the "Donkey" something. He said, 'Do you mean the Don Quixote?' I said yes and couldn't believe it when he said he was staying there too and would take some of my belongings in his bag!

'That's very kind,' said Alison, forcing a smile. I just got a glare before she stomped off down the corridor.

I said, 'It's very decent of you, er…'

'Tony. No problem.'

By this time the priority queue had gone on ahead and we were stuck with the nons.

'Sorry you had to drop out of the Priority Queue,' I said.

'Don't worry about it. We're all going to the same place. Just give me your stuff.'

I grabbed some bits and gave them to him. Then I tied the case with my dressing-gown sash and we headed down the corridor. Alison wasn't speaking to me when I got to my seat. She didn't actually say a word till the steward came along and asked if one of us was capable of opening the exit door in an emergency. Then she confirmed that I could, of course, and he smiled at her. All blokes smile at Alison, even gay ones.

I was surprised at the number of kids on board. I mean, it's flaming September. Weren't they supposed to be back at school? We'd only been seated for five minutes when the family from hell came and sat behind us. Where else? The mother was dressed in a floaty smock with a face full of freckles and curly salt-and-pepper hair. Her son, who wore a bright green baseball cap, was probably about ten. He was also a little twit because, despite his mother telling him not to, he kept kicking my seat. His name was Ethan, probably short for euthanasia (if only). The other child, who Freckles referred to as

Chloe – probably short for chloroform – was about three and kept grizzling for "Bobo" which her mother tried to retrieve from the overhead locker without success. She gave a huff when the steward told her to sit down. He then demonstrated the emergency routine which could not be heard above Chloroform's screaming. It turned out that Euthanasia had been hiding Bobo – a small toy rabbit – all the time. He launched it at the steward just as he was demonstrating how to inflate a life vest with its attached whistle. Bobo hit him right between the eyes. After a "severe" telling off by Freckles – 'Oh, Ethan, that's so naughty!' – Euthanasia began kicking my seat even harder.

Alison had witnessed none of this of course, being engrossed in her magazine and generally oblivious to my discomfort. The business of my burst suitcase was clearly still uppermost in her mind. As well as not speaking she refused to look at me either – charming!

I gazed out of the window and tried to switch off. I thought of Tony offering to help in spite of appearing like the grumpiest man on earth. Talk about the kindness of strangers! I bought wine from the drinks trolley and began to feel quite mellow despite the kicking from behind and Chloroform's whinging, which had resumed, even though Bobo had been located.

I wondered why, in this day and age, a soundproof helmet for keeping kids quiet on flights, or anywhere come to that, hadn't been invented. The *"Kiddie Quiet"* could simply be placed over a child's head and clicked onto a circular collar. Guaranteed to drown even the loudest screeching, it would come in several different designs. Froggie, in green, would have frog eyes on its top; Puss Cat, favoured by little girls, would have furry stick-up ears and whiskers on its front; and Pigger, the unisex model, would have pink floppy ears and a little snout.

I imagined creating the helmets myself and taking them on *Dragons' Den*. Of course there'd be the usual picky questions like cost and envisaged profit margins, projections and forecasts – all of which I'd handle with aplomb. The Dragons would find no loophole in my marketing expertise, that's for sure. I'd explain that accessories were available, like socks and matching rucksacks. Yeah, the sky would be the limit if someone had their head, or rather helmet, screwed on. Hmmm…

All three prototypes would be lined up on the table. No doubt a Dragon would insist on trying one on, only to find they couldn't get it off.

'Well, I did warn you,' I'd say, as someone ran on with a blowtorch. Eventually the Dragon would be released with scorched nose while Deborah tittered.

'I'm out!' they'd cry thankfully.

'Yeah,' I'd reply, 'but what about the *"Kiddie Quiet"*?' Hahaha!! I couldn't help laughing out loud. Alison glared at me again.

I'd been so preoccupied with my invention that I hadn't seen Tony go into the bog. He was just coming out as I took a large glug of wine. I noticed his suit was really crumpled. That's the only thing with linen – it's wrinkly but cool, rather like Tony himself, even though he's getting on a bit. Anyway, I was so busy ogling his trousers that I didn't realise he was looking at me till he'd almost gone past. I raised my plastic tumbler in a toast but he didn't smile. He probably thought I was a right weirdo. First the business with my oversized bag and now here was another oversized bag, namely me, boozing and ogling his groin area like there was no tomorrow.

The weather was boiling when we landed. I felt like a baked spud in my polo-neck sweater. God knows what I was thinking when I put that on. Added to which, the canvas killers were now killing me. Talk about an advert for what not to wear while travelling abroad in summer. I looked around for Tony in case he might want to share a cab, but there was no sign of him.

We were given a glass of bubbly on arrival here at the hotel. Alison told me off for guzzling mine before the porter had arrived to take our luggage. I hoped she wasn't going to keep this up all through the holiday. At home when we fall out, which isn't often admittedly, we give each other a wide berth for a few days. It wouldn't be quite so easy here in Majorca.

We could've carried the bags up here ourselves, or I could've at least, being strong enough to open the emergency doors on the plane, obviously – but Alison was already batting her eyelashes at the porter, Miguel. She tipped him five euros after he drew back the curtains on our amazing view. It's certainly an improvement on the place Roy picked on that last holiday – a three-star all-inclusive with people rolling about sloshed most of the time.

Our room then had overlooked the bar where people were scraping chairs back and forth till the early hours. There was a kiddies' ride underneath the window – a horse with round yellow eyes which neighed all night till I went down and pulled the plug out. Roy was oblivious to all of this, of course, being in a coma most nights till mid-morning. When I asked him if we could change rooms he'd looked baffled and said, 'What for?' I had to get earplugs in the end. What with that and a cockroach in the bathroom the size of a tortoise which came shuffling out every time I sat on the loo, it hadn't exactly been the holiday of a lifetime. All the same, and I know it's stupid, but even after everything that's happened, I still kind of wish Roy was here instead of Alison. Obviously, there's no hope for me whatsoever.

Once unpacked we got ready to go out for dinner. The shower here is great, a full-on deluge that you just stand under – forget about climbing into the bath. My feet had gone from saveloys to hovercrafts. I swear I heard them hiss when the water hit them. I realised my flip-flops were amongst the stuff I'd given Tony. I also found I'd given him a couple of pairs of pants. Great! Now he'd find out what size I wore (marquee). He's probably a bit old in the tooth to care about my undies, although I could be wrong. When I checked with reception he hadn't left anything there, so maybe he was still fondling them or trying them on. He might even have been photographing them to put in some sort of exhibition for all I knew – *Lingerie Through the Ages – from Grannie Panties of the Fifties to Agent Provocateur.* No prizes for guessing which end of the spectrum mine would fall into. I could've called his room but didn't know his surname. Anyway, I didn't like to pester him, especially after crotch-ogling.

'You'll just have to wear the shoes you've got on for now,' said Alison when I told her about the flip-flops, knowing full well I was in pain. 'And God knows why you packed your dressing gown. They actually have bathrobes here, you know.'

I was starting to lose it by then.

'OK, you were right about the bloody shoes,' I said. 'And I'm sorry my case is shit and sorry I packed so much stuff in it. Can we forget about it now?'

Alison said nothing and went to the mini bar. She seemed a bit jittery. I wondered if it had anything to do with "José" from Dartford, but if it did she wasn't letting on. She took out two small bottles of prosecco and handed me one, which I supposed meant a truce. We went out onto the balcony and chinked bottles and talked about where we'd go to eat. Alison suggested an Italian place she knew of about fifteen minutes' walk away. I said could we take a cab but she reckoned it was silly for such a short distance. After looking at the courtesy map of the area, I said what about the beach route so we could paddle our way there, which would have been a lot easier on my feet. Another "no". Alison wanted to wear her pink designer sandals. I'd just have to suffer the canvas killers and buy some more flip-flops for the walk back.

The restaurant, when we got there, was quite impressive with Roman statues and plastic grapevines everywhere. After a bowl of pasta and a couple of glasses of vino I was feeling quite relaxed. Alison even managed a smile or two and our earlier tiff was forgotten.

'Should you be eating that?' she asked when I ordered crème brûlée for dessert. 'I mean, with your lactose thingy…'

'Well, if I can't treat myself on holiday…' I argued, although I knew I was probably risking it.

'Of course,' she said after ordering cheesecake. 'Have whatever you want. It's just that lactose intolerant means lactose intolerant wherever you are in the world by my reckoning.'

'Yes, but it's usually stress that brings it on,' I told her. 'I'm feeling quite chilled now, actually.'

When Joe arrived out of the blue, I realised this had all been arranged beforehand. I suppose I didn't mind really, especially with Alison being keen on him. He was just as I remembered from her photos – tanned with dark hair and those neon teeth.

'José!' she exclaimed. Her eyes were wide with pretend surprise as she stood up to greet him. He made a big show of kissing her on both cheeks and went to do the same to me but I ducked away with the excuse that I needed the loo.

'What did I tell you?' laughed Alison.

I felt like saying, 'Oh, shut up. I only need a wee, actually, if you must know,' but I didn't want to go there in front of Joe.

I sat on the loo studying my face in the mirror on the back of the door wondering how I might improve my look. The light switch was a press-in thing that only stayed on for a few seconds before I was plunged into darkness. I pressed it again, wondering if the glasses should go in favour of contact lenses, but specs did make me look vaguely intelligent. I'd graduated from the NHS pink ones I'd worn in primary school to black frames in my teens and had worn that style ever since. The optician told Mum they gave my face definition. I thought they made me look a bit like the Greek singer Nana Mouskouri, but Mum reckoned it was more like Olive from *On The Buses*.

Back at the table, Joe suggested a nightcap at his place, "Villa Rosa" as he called it. I knew he wanted me there like a hole in the head. The feeling was quite mutual, so I said I was tired and would go back to the hotel.

'Aw, that's a shame,' said Alison pretending to be concerned. 'But it has been a long day for you.'

Yeah, the poor old stooge only along for the ride was knackered. For the second time in the day I felt like whacking her one. As they hugged and kissed, I noticed

Alison's cheesecake lay untouched. I polished it off – shame to waste it.

I wandered off past the brightly lit shops and bars. I bought some new flip-flops and dumped the "canvas killers" in a bin outside the Irish bar. Taking the beach route, I paddled back to the hotel. The moon was shining on the water and I was feeling more relaxed than I had in a long time when, all of a sudden, I felt a familiar twinge in my gizzards. I hoped I had imagined it but no, there it was again. A siren went off in my head like the one in *Alien* when Sigourney Weaver has to load the trolley with vital equipment before the mothership blows up. I speeded my paddling up a bit before breaking into a trot, then a canter. Galloping, like the black horse in the bank ad on TV but not quite so gracefully, I covered the last few yards to the hotel reception, narrowly missing Miguel with a tray of cocktails, and made it to the *aseos* in the nick of time.

Rescue

'Eggs, I'll be bound…'

I turned from watching the chef cooking my omelette to find Tony standing behind me. He was dressed in a blue open-necked shirt and white shorts – his camera slung over his shoulder. I wished I didn't already have two sausages, bacon and hash browns on my plate. He must have thought I was a right gannet. Joe had dropped Alison back to the hotel earlier and she was seated outside on the veranda, eating a bowl of fruit and muesli. She obviously hadn't been asked to stay for breakfast which I thought was a bit off. I asked Tony what he'd meant about eggs.

'They're good for binding you up if you get holiday tum,' he said.

'Oh… er… what makes you think I have?' I asked him. Bloody hell, had he seen me legging it into the bogs last night?

'It's just an old saying, that's all. I've left your stuff at reception by the way. I didn't get in until late.'

'Oh, did your coach do the rounds of all the hotels?' I asked him. 'It's a pain that, isn't it? We got a taxi.'

'I hired a car,' he explained. Of course he had. 'I just had to go out again as soon as I arrived to catch the light.'

'You're a photographer, then?' I asked, realising it was obvious. 'I mean, a professional one?'

'Yes, freelance,' he replied. 'I'm here for a couple of days shooting birds and wildlife.'

'Oh, right. That sounds like fun. We're just here for a week's break. Thanks again for taking my bits – I mean, my things.'

'No problem,' he said as I moved away. 'Have a good day.'

I thought how brilliant it would be to accompany Tony as his assistant for the day, carrying rolls of film maybe, until I realised it's all digital now. I was redundant before I started. Haha! It would have been lovely driving along with him though – my hair blowing in the breeze Grace Kelly style. More like Ned Kelly in my case. I reckoned I'd probably look like something off a key ring by the time I'd finished.

After breakfast Alison went to find a spot on the beach while I finally got my stuff from reception, which included not two, but three pairs of pants, a couple of tops and of course, my flip-flops. Tony had put them in a bag from the tax-free shop, so he'd obviously touched the pants, even if fleetingly. I suddenly felt exposed and a bit upset. If only I'd had more time at the airport to decide what to hand over to him, a complete stranger, but I was in a stress, of course, and not thinking straight. I wouldn't mind if he really was a grumpy old sod, but he's not grumpy at all and quite handsome in his own way with a bit of a twinkle in his eye.

'There you go again,' I said to myself as I tied the straps to my sundress behind my neck – 'Trying to latch onto some poor unsuspecting bastard who wouldn't fancy you gift-wrapped, especially now he's seen your pants. Alison's right; you need to get a life. Look at you! As for Phil back at home – to think he'd ever have been interested in you! Roy was right; you are one big fat cow. He only stayed with you all that time because you were useful on the home comforts front. Then one day he got a better offer and away he went. Why were you so surprised?'

Despite the sun shining through the window and the sounds of people enjoying themselves down in the pool, those old suicidal feelings started to kick in again. What was I still doing here? Why hadn't I topped myself by now? There was still time. I pulled the straps around the front of my neck till the skin puckered. Yeah, why didn't I just garrotte myself there and then and have done with it? Then I thought of the aggro Alison would have in transporting me back to the UK even if a simple cremation was arranged and my ashes put in an urn. She hates having anything too bulky in her luggage and would be sure to kick off.

I let go of the straps and started bawling. The cleaner

chose that moment to come in. She gave me a weird look as I rinsed my face in the sink, probably assuming I was hungover.

'*Que pasa?*' she said. 'You are OK?'

I nodded and quickly slipped out of the door. On the way to the beach I stopped off at the garden bar for a double vodka and tonic to calm myself down. I sat watching a bunch of slim girls in bikinis jumping about in the pool. "The Girl from Ipanema" was playing. I composed my own version:

Big and fat and old and fifty,
The girl called Gloria Grey goes walking
And when she walks each one she passes goes
Ugghhhhh!

When she walks she's like a dump truck
That moves and sways and looks enormous
And as she passes each one she passes goes
Yuuuckkkkkk!

Oh… but I watch her so sadly…
How can I tell her I hate her…?
Oh… lalalalalalalaaaaa…

Another drink would just about do it, I reckoned. The barman looked at me a bit oddly when I got a refill, but I didn't care. I felt like going completely rogue and throwing my plastic tumbler into the pool just for the hell of it. I didn't though and went to join Alison on the beach instead. She was lying with her eyes closed listening to music. There was a green plastic crocodile a couple of feet away. I assumed she must have bought it because she only ever floats and would want to make sure her eye make-up stayed put if she went into the water.

She sat up and asked if I fancied a spa treatment later. I told her I'd seen a Chinese woman doing massage on the beach which was probably cheaper than the spa. Alison corrected me, of course, explaining that Minda was actually Vietnamese. She'd been leaving her card up and down the beach and it was probably best to avoid Minda as she didn't wash her hands between clients.

After Alison had gone back under her earbuds I watched Minda in her coolie hat massaging someone and she did wash her hands afterwards at the shore actually. Alison didn't bloody well know it all as a matter of fact. The vodka had kicked in. Feeling rebellious I called Minda over and said 'Twenty euros?' the way I'd seen her previous client negotiate.

'Twenty onry for back,' she replied. 'Ho body for ferty much better deo.'

I decided I might as well go the whole hog and have the whole hog done. When she first started it was great – really cool on my back. Lovely! I looked across at Alison who was oblivious. It was wonderful having someone's hands – anyone's hands, actually – working on me. All the stresses and strains of the previous few months began to disappear. Minda really seemed to know her onions, which got me thinking about having steak and chips for dinner with onion rings on the side.

It was so peaceful listening to the sea rolling in. I wished it could go on forever until Minda grabbed my left leg, bent it right back and started digging around the base of each toe. This was slightly uncomfortable to start with then bloody excruciating, as if she was trying to pull my toes out one by one. It was obviously some sort of torture method used by the Vietcong handed down by her grandad. I felt like screaming but daren't. Alison was watching now so I just grinned as if I was really enjoying it. Minda finally let go of my leg. I could've cried with relief if it hadn't thumped down so hard bashing my toes, which was sheer agony. After a good thumping of my entire body with her balled fists – probably her way of releasing her feelings about tourists in general – Minda pocketed the thirty euros and moved off in search of another victim.

'Nice?' asked Alison.

'Fantastic,' I said, about to pass out.

'Fancy a walk? They do a nice coffee in the Irish bar.'

'Er… Yeah… sure.'

Rigid with pain I limped across the sand behind her.

'Aren't they your old shoes?' Alison asked when we were seated on the bar's terrace. She pointed to where one of my canvas killers was perched on top of the bin nearby. The other had fallen out and lay on its side next to a couple of empty tins of Guinness Extra Cold.

'You probably ought to have taken them back to the hotel to dump,' she said. 'That bin's an eyesore and you've only added to it.'

'OK, OK…' I said and went to retrieve the horrible things. I knew if I didn't remove them they'd be the only thing Alison would see until we left the bar. I put them in my beach bag out of sight. Before she could lecture me again about the foolishness of buying cheap shoes, I quickly asked if it was too early for a glass of wine. I needed something to take the edge off my sore toes.

'I guess we could treat ourselves,' she said. 'Even though it is a bit early in the day.'

Yessss!

'Well, we are on holiday,' I said. 'Maybe the rules could be bent a little.'

When the waiter came to take our order, I was going to suggest that a bottle would work out cheaper than a couple of glasses but thought the better of it. Instead I asked how her evening went with Joe and whether the spark was still there.

'Oh, definitely,' she said, a bit too quickly. 'He's fantastic. We've got so much in common. We have the same tastes in everything: good food, wine, sailing.'

'Sailing?' I said. 'Has he got a boat then?'

'Yes, it's a speedboat, actually. I'm hoping for a trip in it sometime.'

I thought, *after you got dumped back here at first light, keep hoping.*

'Shame it's such a long-distance relationship,' I said.

'Yes, well, the world's a lot smaller these days. I can be over here in a couple of hours. Anyway, we've agreed to respect each other's space. Nothing kills a relationship more than constantly being together as you well know. Familiarity breeds contempt as they say.'

'Right.'

Of course, I was forgetting – it was all my fault that Roy buggered off. I made the mistake of just being there for him. Luckily, the wine arrived then. Alison took a sip while I took a large glug, promising myself another glass whether she liked it or not.

●

Back on the beach I was just about to doze off when I saw Tony climbing onto a pedalo a few yards away. He hadn't really struck me as a pedalo kind of bloke. He had a pair of binoculars around his neck along with his camera so I reckoned he was probably off to get a few snaps of the coastline. The pedalos were all shaped like swans and had numbers on. Tony's was number seven. I remembered that joke about boats going out on a lake where number sixty-six doesn't come back and the guy calls out "Are you in trouble, number ninety-nine?" Haha! The old ones are the best.

I watched Tony until he rounded the bend beyond the bay and disappeared from view. I dozed off then and woke almost an hour later with a stiff neck and a mouth like the inside of Khruschev's cage. I glugged down some water and noticed that Tony had not returned. The pedalo guy was joking around with a couple of girls and hadn't clocked the absence of number seven. I hoped Tony wasn't in difficulties. What if he'd gone too far out? He wouldn't be able to swim for it and keep his precious camera dry at the same time. Alison was asleep. Her cheeks were puffing in and out, so even though I couldn't hear it from where I was sitting, I knew the usual *Ivor The Engine* chuffing noise was going on.

I grabbed the green crocodile and stumbled into the sea. It was the first time I'd gone so far out since that morning in Hythe back in June and I felt I needed the support. I was feeling dazed and confused and slightly sloshed for some reason. I held on to croccie's little handle and kicked off. I'd gone about a hundred yards before I started to go round the bend. I'm already round the bend, of course, but I made for where the bay ended in an outcrop of rock and swam around it. Then I saw pedalo number seven at the shore of what looked like a private beach. An old hut stood there on supports. A life-saving ring hung beside its door with the name "Villa Rosa" on it. This was Joe's beach, obviously. There was no sign of any speedboat, though.

It was then that I saw Tony at the top of a flight of steps aiming his camera into the bushes. Maybe he'd found a rare bird or some local "flora and fauna". I was about to call out but it occurred to me that he might not appreciate the interruption. I closed my eyes and just floated for a bit. I thought the hissing sound I heard then was the sea rolling over the shore, until I realised that croccie had withdrawn his support and was slowly sinking.

I kicked the useless thing away and splashed about, celebrating the fact that the horrible memories of Hythe were receding. It felt good to be in the blue Med with the sun on my back. Tony turned around and trained his bins on me. I waved and called his name just in case he didn't recognise me in my cozzie and mistook me for Ursula Andress in *Dr No*. My head felt really hot and I ducked under the water, feeling born again. I surfaced in time to see him hurrying down the steps. He obviously felt like a dip too because he took off his bins, his camera and his money belt and dived into the water. I thought it was nice that he wanted to join me. He was probably boiling and needed to cool down. He disappeared under the water for a few moments before bobbing up beside me gasping – his hair all stuck to his face.

'Hang on!' he instructed, slipping an arm around me. 'I've actually done a life-saving course, but it was some time ago...'

'What?' I yelled. 'Tony, I was waving, not drowning!'

'Eh?' he said, pushing his hair out of his eyes. 'But I thought your inflatable thing had gone down and you were in difficulties!'

'Oh, no, no – I'm a good swimmer! I got medals for it at school!'

'Great!' he said, dropping me like a hot, or rather a cold, wet cake. 'That's really good to know…'

I felt a right gonk.

'I think I'm about to pass out,' he said. His eyes were rolling about a bit. 'I feel rather light-headed. It's all those bloody fags.'

'Lie back,' I instructed and grabbing him under the chin, I towed him back to the shore where he collapsed onto the sand.

'Sorry,' he said. 'Caught me unawares.'

'I'm the one who should be sorry, for giving you the wrong idea,' I said as he lay panting. 'I was just enjoying myself. It's been a long time since I had so much fun. Thanks a million for the attempted rescue, even though I didn't need it.'

'Well, I obviously bit off more than I could chew.'

'I hope I didn't disturb your work?'

'I'd heard that Balearic warblers have been sighted around here. They'd make a good shot for a twitcher mag, but I'm sure there'll be another time…'

'This beach belongs to the villa up there,' I told him. 'It's owned by someone my friend's seeing. We'd better go before we're spotted or I won't hear the end of it.'

'Oh, right. Well, you're welcome to share the pedalo.'

'Thanks,' I said and climbed aboard. I was amazed when it didn't lean to one side.

'Why did you venture out so far?' he asked as we pedalled back.

'To tell you the truth, I saw you heading off. You'd been gone quite a while so I thought I'd investigate.'

'Good thinking. These pedalos have been known to go a bit rogue in deep water.'

His face was so serious it made me laugh. I noticed his hair had started to dry and looked like little feathers fluttering in the breeze. I got an idea of how he might've looked when he was a boy.

'Seriously, it was very sweet of you to have been concerned,' he said. 'Do you fancy a drink?'

Silly question. I said OK, I could probably force one down and started pedalling slightly faster. Alison looked gobsmacked when she saw me clambering out onto the beach with Tony. I grabbed my bag and said I'd see her later.

●

We were sitting in the garden café. My cat sarong hid my flab at least and my hair was still damp – not quite so much of a busby as usual. Tony was smoking. He smokes quite a lot, I've noticed – even more than Roy used to before he supposedly gave up, and that's saying something. Sitting there I felt a bit awkward. I don't really know him very well after all and he's so well spoken and clever. It turns out he lives in a village near Maidstone. He asked what I did for a living. I told him I was between jobs after being made redundant from a legal practice a couple of months ago. I didn't mention the word "secretary" as there was just a chance he might assume I was a solicitor.

'Oh, really? What do you specialise in?' he asked.

My professional status was short-lived; I confessed to having been a float secretary for ten years.

'What's a float secretary?'

'One who covers for others when they're away or just helps out,' I told him. 'A general dogsbody, in other words.'

'I prefer "float",' he replied. 'You're good at floating as you demonstrated this afternoon.'

I laughed and so did he between bouts of coughing.

'Seriously, did you never think about becoming a lawyer yourself?'

'Me?' I said. 'I don't think so. I'd have to have a brain for a start.'

'You shouldn't under-sell yourself like that,' he said. 'It's not good for the soul. You obviously have certain talents…'

'Like what?' I said. 'Setting off alarms and getting my case stuck in metal frames?'

I left out the crotch-ogling.

'That can happen to anyone,' he said. 'I set the alarm off too if you remember. I was referring more to your powers of observation. Take today for example, *The Case of the Missing Pedalo*: an exercise in detection followed by a decision to investigate which was admirable.'

'That was just me being nosy,' I told him.

'Sometimes it pays to be nosy,' he said.

'How about you?' I asked. 'Have you always been

interested in photography? I mean, did you always know that's what you wanted to do?'

'I was a teacher for a while, but I gave it up after my wife died a few years ago.'

'Oh, I'm really sorry,' I said.

'I taught English but decided I needed a change after Maisie went.'

'I see… how…? I mean…'

'Cancer.'

'Right…'

'It was a long, protracted illness…'

He looked as if he might say more, then decided not to.

'Any kids?' I asked.

'A son, Barty. He lives in Brighton with his partner. We see each other now and then. Barty does his own thing. He's a lot like me, I guess – apart from being gay. It doesn't matter that he is, of course. I'm just not terribly keen on his partner and tend to make my bi-yearly visit when he's away.'

I didn't really know what to say, so I changed the subject and said I'd like to see his work some time. He picked up his camera and showed me some amazing shots of the sea and boats out on the horizon. There were some beautiful close-ups of tropical birds, which made me feel even more guilty for interrupting him earlier by splashing about like a crazed porpoise. I told him his photos had so much detail in them that if he took a shot of a plane taking off you could probably see people in their seats. He laughed and said he wasn't quite that good. We sipped our drinks and did some people-watching. Tony is very good at sizing people up, it seems. God knows what he thinks of me. A couple came by kissing and laughing. The girl's T-shirt had a cuddly bear on the front with the words "I Saw This and Thought of You" underneath.

I said, 'Oh, God – how naff!'

A sulky teenager followed behind his parents, dragging his feet. Tony reckoned this would more than likely be his last family holiday before he went off to Ayia Napa with his mates. I was just saying that an elderly man in a Union Jack cap limping along with a stick would probably settle for Scarborough next year when who should come bowling up but Freckles, with Chloroform and Euthanasia in tow.

'It was definitely her, Mum!' said Euthanasia, pointing at me. 'It was just lying on the beach where I left it and she picked it up and took it in the sea. I saw her!'

'You owe me twenty euros for my son's plastic crocodile!' said Freckles.

I was about to argue that the crocodile belonged to my friend but realised I had no proof of that.

'If I may,' Tony interrupted. 'I should be delighted to pay you for the crocodile. It certainly served its purpose this afternoon.'

He took his wallet from his money belt.

'I don't care what warped stuff you get up to,' said Freckles. Her face had gone pink. 'To steal a child's brand-new inflatable for the purpose is unacceptable.'

'To be constantly kicked in the back all the way from Gatwick is pretty unacceptable too!' I pointed out, glaring at Chloroform. 'Not to mention the shrieking!'

'I'm not sure if it has occurred to you but these are children!' Freckles was now turning purple. 'That's what they do!'

'Yes, when they're spoilt and have no discipline,' I argued.

'Ladies, please,' said Tony handing her the money. 'Let's draw a line under the matter, shall we?'

Freckles took the money with a huff and walked away. Euthanasia looked back smiling in triumph. I gave him the finger. He told his mum but by the time she turned around, I was scratching my nose instead. I went to pay Tony back but he said it was money well spent to get rid of them and did I fancy another drink.

'Better not,' I said, not wanting him to get the wrong, or rather the right, idea about me.

'Oh, come on, let's push the boat out!'

'Don't you mean the pedalo?' I said. He laughed again and turned to hail a waiter but none was around.

'It's Happy Hour, two drinks for one,' I explained. 'You have to go and queue at the bar – at least, I think that's what you do.'

As if I didn't know.

●

I got the Spanish Inquisition from Alison later, of course.

I told her about the crocodile disintegrating and Tony's attempt to rescue me and how I'd rescued him instead and how we'd been on Joe's beach.

'I'm not sure Joe would appreciate just anyone using his private beach,' she said.

'Tony didn't know it was a private beach, and he wasn't using it as such; he was trying to snap at some birds in the bushes above.'

'Sounds a bit of a perv to me, going around with that camera all the time. What did you find to talk about, anyway?'

'This and that. His work mainly.'

'Well – opposites attract as they say.'

'What do you mean?'

'It's a bit like Henry Higgins and Eliza Doolittle,' she said. 'He's the clever guy and you're…'

'The dumb cockney flower girl. Yes, I do know the plot of *My Fair Lady*,' I told her. 'But I don't think I'd pass for Audrey Hepburn even on a good day. He's just a friendly bloke. I can have male friends without hoping they're gonna tear my clothes off, you know. I mean, what would be the point in that?'

I pictured Tony in a small boat out on the ocean using my pants as a sail.

'Pleased to hear it,' said Alison.

'What's the plan for this evening, anyway?' I asked her. 'You meeting up with Joe?'

'Like I said, we've agreed to respect each other's spaces,' she replied.

I took that as a no.

We ate here in the hotel and I noticed Alison checked her phone a lot and had a couple more glasses of wine than usual, which meant a night of chuffing. I know it'll carry on until she chokes and wakes herself up – I've seen, or rather heard, it before. Perhaps Joe had a sample of it last night and that's why he hasn't called her. Shame, really.

What a weird day it's been. My ego has been given a bit of a boost by the adventure with Tony. How noble of him to come to my "rescue" once again, even though it nearly killed him, haha! What Alison said of *My Fair Lady* was probably a good comparison – except, of course, in my case it would be *My Fat Lady* – best to keep things in perspective.

The Full Monty

Breakfast was nearly finished by the time I got to the dining room this morning. I had to make do with what scraps were left, which was a bit bloody cheeky, actually, considering this is a four-star place. Added to which, the hot water machine had nearly run dry. There was no chance of an omelette either. The chef made a big show of packing up as I approached. It was only half eleven for goodness' sake and they were already laying the tables for lunch. I mean, crikey!

Alison texted saying she was spending the day at Joe's. He'd obviously been in touch. She asked if I fancied going up to the villa for a drink around six thirty? I didn't, but not having anything better to do, I said OK.

I spent a couple of hours at the pool avoiding all inflatable crocodiles. I had salad for lunch with only one glass of wine and no chips – pretty good going for me really. Around six o'clock, I made my way up to the villa, taking the narrow lane that leads uphill from the resort. I pressed the intercom button at the iron gates and a side door swung open. I walked into a driveway with palm trees either side, leading up to the villa. I had to admit, it was very impressive.

Alison was sitting with a drink beside the pool over to the right. Her bikini was drying on a sunbed nearby. She was dressed in a black halterneck dress and her pink sandals. Joe was wearing jeans, an open-necked shirt and his neon smile. On closer inspection I noticed his chest hair was sprinkled with grey and there were quite a few lines on his face.

'What can I get you, Gloria?' he asked, taking the lid off an ornamental trough.

'Bit like Laurence Olivier in *Sleuth*,' I said, but he just looked baffled. I explained that in the film, Laurence Olivier's character keeps his drink in a garden trough.

'She's a bit of a film buff, our Gloria,' said Alison. 'She can tell you who everyone is in them too, she watches so many. I would never have the time...'

I ignored Alison and asked Joe for a vodka and tonic.

'Nice place you've got here,' I told him.

'Lovely, isn't it?' agreed Alison. 'And with its own private beach, too.'

Her and that bloody beach. I mean, get over it!

'Come on, I'll show you around,' she said as if she owned the place (wishful thinking). She led the way along a leafy path to a padlocked gate set back in the bushes. Beyond this was the flight of steps Tony had used the previous day while in search of warblers.

'Lovely!'

I couldn't resist asking what business Joe was in that he could afford all this. Alison explained that he bought run-down places, did them up and sold them on.

'He did the same in London for years before deciding to move out here,' she said. 'He's in the enviable position of not having to get his hands dirty anymore.'

I was tempted to say 'Except when he tints his hair,' but I didn't.

Back on the terrace Joe waffled on about the most interesting parts of the island to see and the best restaurants and how he'd got his eye on this place or that place to renovate. It was showing off for Alison's sake, of course, and she was lapping it up. He'd booked an exclusive restaurant down near the marina and invited me to join them. Alison looked relieved when I said no thanks. I finished my drink and left them to it. Walking back, I wondered if I was being too critical of Joe. Maybe he's fond of Alison after all, but there's something about him I don't like and it's not just the fact that he's a poser.

Tony was sitting on the terrace when I got back to the hotel and called out did I fancy a nightcap? Over a brandy I told him about the visit to the villa and how Alison was so keen on Joe.

'It's unlike her to be bowled over by anyone,' I told him. 'I think he dyes his hair and I'm not sure his teeth are his own. To quote that old joke – his teeth are like stars; they come out at night.'

Tony laughed.

'I don't know that for sure of course, but I wouldn't

be surprised. He's rich and reasonably good looking. Just her type, I suppose. I hope it doesn't end in tears, that's all.'

'Well, she's a big girl now,' said Tony. 'I'm sure she'll work it out for herself. What about you? What's your type?'

I said I didn't have one. Then, I found myself telling him about Roy and the years of wasted life.

'Ten years is a long time to be with someone,' he said.

'I blame myself,' I told him. 'I was far too accommodating for way too long. I don't expect Tessa was the first. I should have thrown him out years ago. I'm an idiot.'

'Far from it,' said Tony. 'Although you can be rather annoying…'

'What do you mean?' I said.

'I mean, putting yourself down all the time, especially when you're witty and clever…'

'And tall and fat,' I said without even thinking.

'There you go again,' he said. 'Stand up.'

'What?' I said.

'Come on, stand up.'

I stood up.

'You're exactly the same height as me, five foot ten. Most models are that, at least.'

'Models for jumbo fashions maybe,' I said.

'Stop it. Now, hold out your arms.'

I held them out obediently.

'Pure muscle,' he said, squeezing them. 'No fat that I can see.'

'And this?'

I grabbed a handful of my belly thinking he might as well have the full monty as he'd come this far. He put his cigarette between his lips, pushed my hands out of the way and squeezed.

'Again, muscular is the word. No fat there – hard as a rock. You're a powerful woman, Grey. Look how you dragged me out of the sea yesterday. I felt I was in very safe hands – er… arms.'

I didn't know what to say. In fact, I felt quite choked. I sat down, took a sip of brandy and gazed out to sea.

'As for your relationship with Ray…'

'Roy,' I corrected.

'Sorry. Roy. OK, it didn't work out but you mustn't look on it as a waste of life. Learn from it. There's no point in constantly looking back wishing you'd done things differently. We can all do that but it doesn't change anything. We just have to keep going and try not to make the same mistakes. You gave him ten years; don't give him any more.'

I suppose he was right. I thought for a moment he was going to tell me about his own experiences but he didn't. We just sat there looking out at the lights on the water with neither of us speaking for a while. Somehow it didn't feel uncomfortable.

It was silly, but I didn't really want him to leave first, even though I barely know him. After a while, I said I was a bit tired and toddled off. From the balcony up here I could see him sitting on the terrace, one floor below. I could smell his cigarette smoke as it drifted up. I imagined he was thinking about his wife and the holidays they'd had together. I stayed watching until he eventually got up and moved away.

Banged Up Abroad

Alison texted from the villa this morning to say she would be staying for lunch with Joe. I went off to the beach and was just enjoying the second of two small bottles of prosecco hidden in my bag, when she turned up looking a bit disgruntled. Apparently lunch was off. Joe had got a phone call about a property which he had to see right away.

'Oh, well if he's working…' I said. 'And you did say you were respecting each other's spaces.'

'I would've liked a bit more notice, that's all,' she replied crossly before plugging in her music and turning away. She was in a "strop" and for a good reason. I couldn't do anything to help so I decided to leave her to it and go for a swim.

I set off to Joe's beach for the hell of it. The sea felt lovely – no crocodile needed. I remembered what Tony had said about me being strong and that he felt safe in my arms. I suppose I am strong if I think about it. I just need to use the word "muscular' rather than "fat" and do what he suggested. Stop putting myself down basically. Easier said than done, but worth a try, I guess.

I'd just rounded the bay when I caught sight of Joe and a young blonde girl in a bikini climbing out of a speedboat. I quickly drew in behind the rocks. So, this was the property he had to see. It was clearly a hot one. She looked young enough to be his daughter. They kissed and hugged as they made their way towards the villa steps.

When I thought it was safe, I got out of the water and climbed up after them. I had to know what was going on here for Alison's sake. Through the bushes, I watched as the girl splashed about in the pool, while Joe chopped two lines of coke. Blimey! A few moments later the girl climbed out and joined him in snorting the stuff, before sitting in his lap and snogging him. (Ugh!) He picked her up and took her into the changing room nearby. I felt like a bit of a peeping Tom and was about to leave when there was a fluttering in the bushes behind me. I turned to see a little grey bird with an orange beak. A couple of moments later another one joined it. I wondered if these were the warblers Tony had been hoping to see before he was so rudely interrupted. I stood watching them for a few minutes thinking how sweet they were and how their lives are so uncomplicated.

I was so busy in warbler world that I hadn't noticed Joe and his girlfriend heading in my direction. Blimey, I thought, that must've been a quickie! Hahaha! I belted back down the steps, hearing their laughter close behind me. I was frantically trying to think of an explanation for being there when I noticed the door to the beach hut was open and quickly dived inside.

I crouched down behind the door. Peeping around it, I could see the girl making for the speedboat. It looked as if Joe was about to join her, but then he turned towards the hut. I thought for one awful moment he might have seen me dash inside and was about to ask what the hell I was playing at. I squatted even further down trying to make myself small, which is difficult at the best of times. He'd obviously just forgotten to shut the door because suddenly it swung closed. Everything went dark and I heard the sound of a bolt being drawn across.

A few moments later, I heard the speedboat's engine starting up. Looking through the hut's tiny window, I saw Joe at the wheel and the girl waving her arms in the air, shrieking with delight as the boat cut through the water.

Forcing myself to stay calm, I tried to work out what to do. I remembered that the hut was raised up on supports and when my eyes became more accustomed to the light, I saw that the floor was rotten with holes in several places. I reckoned if I could just make one of the holes bigger and squeeze through into the space beneath it I'd be laughing. Actually, no – if anything, I'd be crying – especially if I got stuck. I was wearing only my swimsuit, but there was nothing for it – the only way was down. I looked around for something to smash through the timber, but all that hung on the wall were a pair of flippers and a couple of fishing nets. It was no good; I'd just have to rely on my own two feet. I found the biggest hole and started kicking the wood around it for all I was worth. A few minutes and many splinters later, I'd made a space big enough to crawl through.

I went in head first, pushing myself a little at a time. I felt like screaming when the jagged wood scraped against my skin. I managed to get my shoulders through, but the rest of me was wedged tight. What a way to go! After all my carefully planned suicide attempts, my life was to end here, wedged through the floor of a beach hut with my bottom in the air – a fitting end some might say.

I was absolutely dying to pee. When I got as far as pushing my hips through, a centimetre at a time, the pressure on my bladder was absolute hell. I hadn't wet myself since I was a kid and I wasn't going to start now. Gradually, I wormed my way out onto the sand. I lay there panting like a newly born calf before turning onto my back and shuffling along towards the rear of the hut. At last I felt the hot sun on my face. Hallelujah! My head was free but the rest of me was stuck. I lay there helpless for what seemed like hours, unable to turn away from the blazing heat.

I felt a long, wet tongue licking my face. Ugh! Someone was calling 'Tito! Tito!' I tried to shoo the dog away but my mouth was parched and my lips were stuck over my teeth like a crocodile's. That animal seemed determined to feature in my life one way or another.

More wetness all over my face. I closed my eyes thinking that Tito might have decided to treat me to a golden shower until I realised it was just water I was being sprayed with.

'Grey! Open your eyes,' said a familiar voice.

Obviously, I'd got sunstroke and was delirious because for one crazy moment I thought the voice belonged to Tony.

'Come on, drink!'

'Tony, is it really you?' I stammered. 'How… what are you doing here?'

'I might ask you the same question,' he replied. 'Get this down you.'

Between gulps of water I explained how I'd been nosing at Joe and his girlfriend and got locked in.

'If Joe thought I'd seen him sniffing coke, he wouldn't be too happy,' I said. 'Then he locks the bloody door and goes off with Barbie in the speedboat. I've been stuck here for ages.'

'Let's see. If I grasp you under the arms, do you think you could push really hard with your feet?'

I told him I'd try. A few minutes later, after a great deal of effort from both sides, the rest of me was free.

'It's a girl, Mrs Grey,' quipped Tony.

'Very funny.'

I struggled to stand up.

'By the way, I think I might've seen a couple of those birds you were on about up there.'

'Where? I've been looking for the past hour or so and zilch. You're sure they were warblers?'

'Grey with red eyes and an orange beak?'

'Ah, that'll be the Balearic, although that description fits you too at the moment, if I may say so.'

'Very funny,' I said. 'Now, would you mind turning your back. I'm about to pee for England.'

Back to Reality

I didn't see Tony again until two days later when I passed through reception on my way to breakfast. He was dressed in his linen suit, which looked slightly less crumpled than the last time I'd seen it, so I reckoned he must have given it a press.

He was waiting for a taxi and explained that he had to get back home for work reasons. He mumbled something about having dinner as he shook my hand. I said that would be nice and that it was good to meet him and pity I hadn't had my camera on me when I'd seen the pair of warblers that day. Afterwards, I thought what a silly thing to have said. I mean, as if I'd have been able to capture them in anything like the quality Tony produced, even if I'd happened to have a waterproof camera tucked down my swimsuit or strapped to the front of my head.

He just smiled and said I should try and keep out of trouble and to enjoy the rest of the stay. I waited for him to ask for my number, but he didn't – of course he didn't.

Why would he? I've only known him five minutes. Yeah – I'm actually learning! Besides, it's unlikely anyone could compete with his wife in his affections, least of all a dumb, big-knickered, fat – I mean muscular – heifer like me. He'd be a good friend though, I reckon – dependable. Someone you could call at a time of crisis. Maybe that's why he didn't give me his number, to make sure I don't. His taxi came then. He got in and I watched as it swung out of the drive and sped away up the dusty road.

●

We came home ourselves a couple of days later. Alison didn't see Joe again before we left. He texted that he'd got caught up in work stuff and to have a safe trip back. She tried to act like she didn't care, but I could tell she was disappointed. I saw her checking her phone a few times. I kept quiet about what I'd witnessed, not sure whether it would have made matters worse.

The flight was delayed an hour but I eventually arrived home to find flowers and a thank-you note from Phil who'd moved out the previous day. I didn't feel quite so upset as I thought I would, especially as he'd left his address and said I should call round for a coffee sometime.

I picked Mog up from the cattery. Apparently, she'd hidden under her blanket for most of the week pining. I doubted it was for me – more likely to be her usual surroundings that she missed. When I let her out of the carry-case she rubbed herself against me, which usually means she wants food. I was surprised when after I fed her, she followed me about and lay next to me on the sofa. She put her head on one side and then stretched out a paw to me, as if she'd decided I wasn't so bad after all.

Alison came round later on after she'd unpacked her case and done her washing. My bag still stood mouldering in the hall with the dressing-gown sash tied around it. We had lunch and looked at photos from Majorca on her tablet thingy. When she saw a selfie of her and Joe beside the pool at the villa, there were a few tears and some flapping of fingertips.

'I'll give it a couple of days and call him,' she decided. 'Like I said, it's easy enough for me to just pop over.'

I was astonished.

'Pop over where? Majorca?'

'Why not?'

'Alison, this is so unlike you,' I said. 'It's usually me that behaves like a wombat.'

'I know it's hard for you to understand, Gloria, but we do have something special, Joe and I.'

I noticed "José" had disappeared and he was now plain Joe.

'I wonder what that can be,' I said. 'I mean, you were in Majorca for seven days and you saw him for what… two of them?'

'He was working. I just happened to arrive during a particularly busy time, that's all. He did warn me.'

This was definitely my cue to tell her about Barbie and the speedboat and how I'd got locked in the hut, but of course she only took in the first bit.

'You're lying!' she said. 'You just didn't like him, that's all!'

'Why would I lie about something like that?' I asked her. 'No, I don't like him particularly and I was hoping you'd drop him as a waste of time when he didn't get in touch.'

'But we got on so well the last time I went there. We've been texting back and forth ever since.'

'Bottom line, Ali,' I said. 'Did he actually suggest you go over?'

'Not in so many words, but I thought once we saw each other again, the flame might be rekindled as they say. Obviously, I was wrong.'

'And you being such a good judge of character where men are concerned too…'

I couldn't help rubbing her nose in it a little bit after what she'd said about me and Roy and familiarity breeding contempt. It was quite hurtful.

'The thing is, Ali, you've got used to calling the shots. Not many guys have let you down. I reckon you only want Joe because you can't have him and it hurts to be dissed, I know.'

'You're right,' she said drying her eyes. (Blimey, that was a first!) 'I can't compete with the likes of Barbie, whoever she is. I have to face facts. I'm forty, not twenty, no matter how good I might look.'

'You look absolutely brilliant,' I assured her. 'You're still young! Age has got absolutely nothing to do with it as you're always telling me.'

'I suppose he sees her all the time,' she went on. 'I just wish he'd told me before I went over there and made a fool of myself.'

'He's a bloke, don't forget, and not likely to pass up an opportunity. He's no spring chicken either and probably going for it while he can. I doubt any self-respecting air head would look twice at him if he wasn't loaded. Money is a great aphrodisiac, as they say.'

It sounded like I spoke from experience. As if. The nearest I'd got to being turned on by dosh was if Roy had splashed out and brought a curry home. Bungle would then have slipped into something silky and become Miss Piggy, running her fingers through Roy's hair and pouring nightcaps in the hope of rounding off the evening with further spiciness, often to no avail.

'Anyway, looking on the bright side, you might have had a lucky escape. I mean, if he's into drugs, who knows? He might've started grooming you to be a mule like on *Border Control*.'

'I don't think that was ever the plan, Gloria.'

'Seriously. He could've tricked you and before you knew it, hidden something in your case.'

'I can't imagine Joe as some Mr Big in a drug cartel. He probably just uses cocaine for recreational purposes because he can afford it. Anyway, he'd be wasting his time tricking me into being a mule. My case is always neat and tidy and I'd jolly well know if anything had been planted in it.'

'Yes, but mules have been known to carry drugs inside their bottoms and sometimes the bag bursts and there's an almighty explosion with loads of poo and white powder everywhere.'

Her face began to crack a bit then.

'Gloria, I don't pretend to be an authority on mules as you obviously are but I doubt it works like that,' she said. 'Surely the person would just implode and die on the spot if they were stupid enough to carry the stuff that way in the first place.'

'They do sometimes, actually,' I told her. 'They're desperate. Anyway, you don't need that shit. You don't need him either. To give you the same advice as you're always giving me, you need to put it all behind you and move on. Fancy a post-hol prosecco?'

She nodded and blew her nose.

We were on our second glass and our ship was back on an even keel as they say, when my phone buzzed. I noticed I had a couple of missed calls from Mum.

'Oh, there you are,' she said. 'I've been trying you all morning.'

Her voice sounded strange. I thought she'd got a cold until I realised she was crying.

'What's up?' I asked.

'It's Kit…'

'What about her?'

'She's dead.'

It was a stroke. Kit had gone down to her recycling bin and collapsed. It had happened two days ago – on Wednesday. Sam, the next-door neighbour, had set off for work in the morning and found her slumped across the lid. He'd thought she was having trouble closing the bin and went to give her a hand before he realised she was unconscious. He'd had no idea how long she'd been there – hopefully not overnight. His wife, Felicity, had called an ambulance and then phoned Mum. Kit had been taken to hospital and slipped peacefully away that evening. Mum said she hadn't called me as I was due home today anyway. She'd told Bev not to call me either, saying I might as well enjoy myself for another day or two and there was nothing I could have done anyway. Maybe not, but I would have known at least.

I didn't press the point because Mum then broke down. Between sobs she said she should have insisted that Kit get an emergency button for around her neck. I said it wouldn't have done much good if she'd been in the throes of the stroke. Then Mum went hysterical and started yelling, 'Oh, God! Kit... Kit!' as if she was the one on the receiving end of the shocking news and could I come to Folkestone straight away as Bev had left to sort the kids.

I drove to Folkestone feeling numb. Even though I knew something awful had happened my brain wouldn't process it. I arrived to find Mum lying on the sofa with a box of tissues beside her. George came in with a tray of tea and patted Mum and then his hair and then Mum again. I knew I should probably hug her but it was difficult – particularly as she was lying down. She didn't meet me halfway either, so I just bent over and nudged her chest with my forehead like a pony.

I patted her leg and said surely she wouldn't have wanted life to drag on for Kit, especially if she'd suffered brain damage from the stroke and wasn't it funny how Kit had been saying that stuff about "seeing" Uncle Jack recently? Mum said there was nothing funny about it. I said I meant funny "peculiar" and not funny "haha" – as if I needed to explain that and where exactly was Kit by the way? Mum couldn't get her breath, so George explained that she was in the hospital mortuary until her body could be released to the undertakers. This would need a doctor's signature and as they were a bit short-staffed it might not happen right away.

Mum asked if I would go and get Kit's belongings from the hospital as she couldn't face it. In a voice that came out like a croak, she said she hoped they'd done everything they could for Kit. I wanted to make her feel better in any way I could, so I said what could they have done any differently? She said operate maybe and that hospitals were all too fond of neglecting the elderly in favour of younger people who had more of a chance. I said Kit probably wouldn't have survived an operation even if one had been suggested. Added to which, she'd told me once that if anything like this happened she wanted to be DLR.

'You mean DNR – do not resuscitate,' said Mum. 'DLR is the Docklands Light Railway, dear.' She still had to be picky even at a time like this.

I drove over to the hospital a bit later. It felt strange, as if I was doing this in slow motion for someone I didn't know – not my auntie who'd been there all my life.

While waiting for Kit's things I took a stroll along the corridor. Someone passing away was just routine here, just like someone being born or someone else being diagnosed with a terminal disease and not surviving and another person making it. I glanced through a window to the floor below where I could see a long metal table with a sink at one end. It looked like where they laid people for inspection prior to sliding them into the freezer. I thought, *blimey – you'd think they wouldn't make the mortuary quite so visible*. Even though it might be all in a day's work to the staff, this was a bit much. It was a good thing Mum hadn't come with me – she'd have freaked out completely.

A few minutes later, a nurse arrived with a brown paper bag containing Kit's items. I signed for them after proving my identity with my driving licence, although why anyone would want to make off with Kit's nightie and sponge bag, I couldn't think. But then of course there were her valuables. The nurse handed me an envelope containing Kit's glasses, her watch and her wedding ring. It was the ring that brought things home to me. It had been on her finger since the day she'd got married to Uncle Jack. It had been there as she'd measured out sweets for me in Woolworths all those years ago and on the day she'd rested her hand, light as a feather, on my own the last time I'd seen her.

I walked towards the exit clutching the paper bag. Tears began to run down my cheeks and I felt faint. I slumped against the window above the room where I'd seen the metal table, imagining Kit lying on it, small and alone, only a couple of days before. I halted mid-sob as I noticed a pair of blue-gloved hands putting salad onto plates lined up for the purpose. I sloped off, turning into the corridor just as the dinner trolley emerged from the lift. A porter had brought it up from the kitchen below. It's amazing how the eye can be deceived in times of stress.

I took Kit's things back to Mum. George had gone out for a round of golf to give us some space. Mum slipped Kit's wedding ring on and talked sadly about how she'd been her bridesmaid when she'd married Jack at twenty-one and how it was a shame they didn't have any kids of their own. She said Kit had miscarried one and no others had come along after that. Kit had actually told me this once but I pretended to be shocked at the revelation all the same.

'She was supposed to go back and have herself checked but never did,' Mum said. 'Poor Kit. It must've been a lonely life without kids.'

She started crying again and choked on her tea which went down her jumper and skirt.

'I'm sorry, Gloria,' she said. I told her there was no problem and quickly wiped up the mess.

'No, I meant sorry for bringing up the subject of kids when you haven't got any yourself. I wasn't thinking.'

This was a bit of a surprise. I told her I'd never really wanted any, not being the mothering kind. Then I thought of how I'd mothered Roy and had tried to look after Phil, so maybe I was deluding myself. Tony wouldn't have needed mothering, of course. He had launched a wonderful career in spite of being widowed. He was self-sufficient, had a posh camera and was quite his own man in every way, it seemed to me. Mum then went on about how the funeral would need to be arranged and Kit's house would have to be cleared out and put on the market and how she didn't know where to start. I said not to worry, Bev and I would sort it all. Then I remembered Khruschev and told Mum of my promise to Kit about taking the budgie.

'If you'd rather have him,' I said, 'you only have to say.'

'No thanks,' she replied. 'You're welcome to the ghastly thing.'

Goodbye

The weather was chilly but bright for the funeral today. There weren't many in attendance at the crematorium, most of Kit's friends having gone on ahead. A couple of old guys who'd known Uncle Jack in the railway works turned up. One was propped up with sticks, the other in a wheelchair. Kit's next-door neighbours Sam and Felicity came and an elderly couple who used to live near to the post office across the green.

'She always spoke,' they said of Kit, but that seemed about the limit of the relationship.

There was an ancient lady called Violet who'd known Kit since they were kids. She said I was looking well and sorry to hear I'd lost my husband and that Charlie was a nice man. I realised she thought I was Mum. Darren took the morning off work to mind the kids so that Bev could attend and Alison came along for support. She'd sorted the buffet and set it out in the kitchen for which I was grateful. No way could I have got my head around it.

The hearse pulled up and the coffin was taken out by four pall-bearers – immaculately dressed, shoes shining.

Death, where is thy sting?

Dunno why that popped into my head then. Then I remembered it came from a verse of "Abide With Me". I'd found a set of old Victorian postcards in Kit's dining room drawer one rainy afternoon. Each card had a picture of people in mourning with a verse underneath. I know how the tune goes because Roy had always watched the FA Cup final and it was sung at the start. I wonder why it hasn't been replaced with something like "What a Wonderful World" even though it isn't.

I'd managed to organise the music at least as Mum was at a loss. She said to choose something cheerful. I knew Kit has been fond of Glenn Miller, so I chose "Chattanooga Choo-Choo". It was playing as Kit was taken in and placed before a set of red velvet curtains. We followed and took our seats. I noticed Mum was glaring at me for some reason.

The celebrant (not that there was much to celebrate) didn't have much to say about Kit except that she'd been a loving sister, which Mum had written on a piece of paper and handed to him just before the service. I probably should have written something too but I couldn't think of anything. Kit was my aunt and meant loads of things to me that I couldn't have put in writing. The celebrant had more to say about Uncle Jack who'd been a shop steward in the railway factory and had often spoken up for workers' rights. I'd noticed the two old workmates sharing their memories of him with the celebrant prior to the service.

Afterwards we all lingered outside looking at the flowers with Mum thanking everyone for coming and inviting them back to mine. I read the condolence cards and earwigged on conversations. The old workmates weren't going to bother with the buffet apparently. The one with the stick said it wasn't Jack's funeral, after all. The one in the chair said, 'Wasn't it? Who's was it then?' The one with the stick said it was Jack's wife's. He'd forgotten her name but it would come to him in a minute.

I'd got sherry in for the elderlies but the four bottles of prosecco in the fridge disappeared rather quickly instead. Felicity got a bit pissed and emotional. She and Sam had been hippies back in the seventies when they'd first moved in. Mum said that Kit and Jack had been worried in case they'd smoked "that pot stuff" or played loud music. As it was, they'd turned out to be quiet and into peace and love, floating about in kaftans and beads. Before she got off her face, Felicity said she was concerned about who might now move into Kit's house when it was sold and she hoped it wasn't foreigners – all peace and love having long since gone out of the window apparently.

Mum was completely spaced out and George made himself useful on drinks duty. Alison had done a good job of the "Finger Buffet" as she called it, which reminded me of when that finger was found in the chips in *The Hitcher*. I told her I was grateful for the profiteroles as they had a calming effect on me.

I said, 'I think it's called mindfulness.'

After I ate six of them Alison said no, that was just greediness.

●

With the funeral out of the way and after a respectful distance of two weeks, Bev and I began helping Mum to clear Kit's house so it could be put on the market after Christmas. The two of us ended up doing most of the clearing while Mum dawdled about, gazing at ornaments and photographs, tearfully reminiscing on their history. We emptied cupboards and drawers full of junk that Kit had accumulated over the years.

Mum's plan after the house got sold was to move from the Folkestone flat in its Victorian block to a more modern place. Bev and I would get "a little something" from the sale. We were grateful but laughed to ourselves that we probably wouldn't be able to retire on it.

In the wardrobe were a couple of funny old dresses in crimplene dating back to the sixties and a few cardigans. Kit's shoe collection was a pair of sensible lace-ups, some sturdy beige sandals and a pair of fur-lined boots which I hadn't seen her wear for years. She hadn't gone out much recently – only to the corner shop with her wheelie if the weather was fine or just down to that bloody bin. I took a couple of faded photos from the bedroom windowsill. One was of Kit and Jack in Folkestone dated July 1960 – the other had been taken at a railway Christmas do. They were smiling in party hats. There were plates of sandwiches on the table, sliced Swiss rolls and chocolate marshmallows.

I took out some flowery cotton undies from the chest of drawers, some thick tights and an unopened pair of summer ones in American Tan which looked prehistoric from their packaging. There were also a few old coins and a couple of half-filled books of Green Shield stamps. Kit's jewellery consisted of a pearl necklace and one made of crystal still in its box. I gave them to Mum which set her off. She collapsed onto the sofa clutching them to her chest as she tearfully recalled long-ago events where Kit had worn them.

I cleared out the cupboard under the kitchen sink. It was full of crap – an old bottle of Windolene, a corroded tin of Brasso, a few decomposed scouring pads and some sponge cloths dried into hard shapes. Seeing these everyday things upset me more than anything. Kit had also started to shrivel and fade and now she was gone. On the back shelf were a couple of cracked old vases, an ancient carton of Ajax and a sink plunger minus its stick. I laughed through tears at the sight of it. That was Kit all over – she threw nothing away.

I went to the understairs cupboard for the vacuum cleaner that Mum had bought Kit a couple of Christmases ago. An old upright one still stood beside it. Kit hadn't thrown this out (just in case). I moved it aside, accidentally knocking a cardboard box from the shelf. I picked up Christmas cards, letters and old utility bills that had spilled out. As I went to replace the box on the shelf to go through later, I picked up an A4-sized manila envelope that had been lying underneath. It was stamped from a law firm in Folkestone. My name had been written across it in black marker pen.

I studied the envelope for a moment remembering what Kit had said about there being something for me in the understairs cupboard. I'd assumed she was wandering in her mind and had thought no more about it. Inside was what looked like her will. I knew Mum had a copy. It had been drawn up fifteen years ago in 2004, shortly after Dad died. At the time Mum had said something about Kit being very kind in providing for her in the future now that she was a widow herself.

I thought maybe Kit had wanted me to have this copy to look after for some reason, although I couldn't think why. I noticed that a letter from the Wills and Probate department was clipped to it, dated more recently in 2007, enclosing with pleasure "the amended Last Will and Testament of Mrs Katherine Mossop".

I was just about to call out to Mum when something stopped me. Amended? I'd turned the pages of the will and found the amendment referred to. Kit had left her house to me.

●

'Oh, well I'm not surprised,' said Mum after she stopped screaming, having been extremely surprised. 'You were always her favourite. You've even taken precedence over me, her own sister. I don't think she could have been right in the head at the time, changing the will like that. I was to have the house and what little money she had was to be divided up equally between the three of us. In fact, looking at the date, I think it was around then that she started to lose it. We'd probably have a case if we got in touch with her GP. I mean, she obviously didn't know what she was doing...'

'I think she knew perfectly well, Mum,' interrupted Bev gently. 'Poor Gloria's never managed to get on the property ladder. Maybe that played on Auntie's mind.'

'Well, that's Gloria's own fault,' replied Mum as if I wasn't in the room. 'The first thing she should've done was buy her own place rather than supporting spongers like Roy Chislett for years.'

I felt awful and offered to sell the house and split the money three ways. At the same time the prospect of owning my home without any need for lodgers or doing boring jobs was becoming more appealing by the minute – a large comfort blanket settling over my chest, but I didn't dare show any enthusiasm.

'No, Auntie Kit left it to you and that's that,' said Bev. 'You deserve it. You were always looking in and doing things for her. She obviously appreciated that and this is her way of showing it.'

'Well, it's all a bit too sneaky if you ask me,' said Mum. 'For all I know, you might've engineered it.'

I said, 'What? How?'

'Always fawning over her. You know how elderly people are. They respond to that sort of thing and before you know it they've left everything to the home help.'

I felt like I'd been punched in the gizzards.

'Or a partner who they've only known for five minutes!'

I didn't know this for a fact, but I felt so hurt I couldn't help it.

Mum's face was crimson. 'How dare you!' she yelled. 'What I do with my estate will be my own affair!'

'Exactly! Just like Kit's was hers.'

'Look, let's all calm down,' said Bev. 'This whole thing's getting out of control. Let's all just be thankful we have our own homes – all three of us when things are so hard for lots of people.'

'I'm still going to have this checked out!' said Mum. 'My own sister!'

She picked up a cushion and began sobbing into it, sending Kit's prized jewels hurtling to the floor.

Boxing Day

I hadn't seen Mum since the ruckus over Kit leaving me the house and wouldn't have been surprised if I'd been excluded from the annual Christmas lunch at her flat yesterday. It would have been a relief really, especially if she was going to kick off about it again, but she sent a message via Bev that I was expected as usual. I still wasn't sure of what kind of reception I'd get, so I thought I'd better be a bit humble. I gave her a kiss when I arrived, wished her a Merry Christmas and said I was sorry about everything. She just told me to hang up my coat properly rather than leave it on the hall chair and we'd say no more about it. Even though this implied that the inheritance was somehow still my fault, I could at least move in to Kit's house in January with a happier heart.

Bev fought a losing battle trying to keep the kids quiet. The girls played around the flat talking to each other on walkie-talkies; Kevin ran about "stabbing" people with a sword that inverted itself on contact (a present from me); and Matty sat texting on his mobile (also a present from me).

After a couple of large sherries Mum was in a world of her own. George brought in a bottle of fizz which Darren declined, saying it was for poofs and he only drank beer. George returned to the kitchen and came back a few moments later with a tin of lager and an electronic carving knife. I wasn't sure if it was meant for the turkey or Darren.

We all wore hats – not the coloured paper variety but the more deluxe "character" version that Mum always goes in for. George's "Napoleon" one was a bit too big and slipped down over one ear, making any hair-smoothing difficult. He made a toast to "absent friends", which set Mum off. Bev dished up Christmas pudding, reminding us all to make a wish. I didn't waste my time – pigs might fly.

I drove through Hythe on the way home. On passing the "Berck-Sur-Mer" sign, I thought how the berk has moved on since that morning back in June. I'll shortly be moving into my own home and my future is clearly mapped out. I may find another job, something part-time in a shop, perhaps – not out of necessity, just for something to do until I retire. I'll sell the house eventually in favour of a small flat as climbing stairs will start to get difficult. When I can no longer look after myself, I'll go into a home if I'm lucky. (Bev might put in a word.) Then I'll pass away quietly and be boxed up and sent on like Auntie Kit. It's all there on the horizon.

Alison had gone to lunch with her parents in New Romney and texted that she'd left my present beside the back door. It turned out to be a stylish travel bag. The card read "*Will fit metal frame at airports*". Haha!

Babe was on TV. I'd never seen the film and it turned out to be quite sad. I started bawling when the little pig sat patiently waiting for the farmer to shoot him. He was spared, of course. It was unlikely he'd be blown to smithereens in a kids' film. Anyway, pigs are killed by electricity in abattoirs, aren't they? I hope it's humane. I remember seeing a documentary when a group of little piglets had followed each other quite happily into a cart, taking them to one of those very places. Unlike Babe they wouldn't have been spared and were probably snuffed out before the little things knew what was happening to them. The fate of the average pig is enough to make you turn veggie. I decided to throw out the bacon from the fridge as soon as possible.

After the film I sat there on the sofa thinking about Auntie Kit and how she was at Mum's on Christmas Day last year and how I'd driven her home afterwards and she'd talked about Christmases in the old days when Jack was alive. Then I just curled up and bawled my eyes out. When I eventually sat up and blew my nose, I noticed that Mog had appeared on the arm of the sofa and was gazing at the TV, as if to let me know she was there.

I slept late this morning and enjoyed a special Boxing Day breakfast of sausage, eggs and – forgetting my vow to Babe – bacon. Unfortunately, that's the way of the world, even for little pigs with fringes. I'd just finished eating when the doorbell rang. I thought it had to be Alison back from her parents but it turned out to be Tony. I just stood there looking at him. Thank God I was dressed at least.

'Sorry to disturb,' he said. 'I've been abroad on another job, then to Barty's for Christmas. Mercifully, his partner had gone to his folks in Wales. I was on my way home and thought I'd just drop by.'

'Oh… right…'

I was trying to think of something witty to say, but nothing came to mind. I was too stunned.

'Wondered if you fancied a curry later?' he said. 'I mean… if you're not busy?'

The last time I'd seen him he'd had on his linen suit and his hair had been fairer from the sun. Now here he was in winter, looking distinguished in a navy overcoat and scarf. There was an expression in his eyes that I couldn't quite read.

'No… I'm not busy,' I said when I found my voice. 'That'll be nice. Er… how did you know where to find me?'

'It was a triumph in detection actually,' he said. 'If I hadn't gone in for photography, I'd probably be with MI5. I remembered the address on your luggage label when I removed it from the frame at the airport.'

'Oh, yes. I'd forgotten about that.'

I hadn't really, but Majorca had kind of faded into the background since Auntie Kit had gone.

'So, how are you?' he said. 'Have you been keeping out of mischief?'

I told him about Kit and how she'd left me her house. He said, "Oh, God, sorry," and that no one was exempt and "we knew not the hour".

After a respectful pause he said it was good I got the house. It would be a fresh start for the new year and he'd pick me up at seven o'clock if that was OK?

I told him that would be fine.

'I've got a few things to do,' he said. 'I'll see you later. Oh, by the way…'

He took a small package from his coat pocket and handed it to me.

'Happy Christmas. Bit late, I know, but…'

'Oh, no,' I said. 'I'm sure it's… er… lovely…'

I didn't want to embarrass either of us by opening it there and then, so I just mumbled thanks and closed the door. I probably should have invited him in for a coffee but I couldn't handle it. I needed some space to take this all in.

After he'd gone I sat down at the kitchen table for a long time just staring at the package before I finally opened it. I took out a small gift box and an expensive-looking Christmas card with an angel blowing a trumpet in gold on the front. Above it were the words "Gloria In Excelsis".

Inside, Tony had written "*I saw this and thought of you*".

I opened the box and took out a brooch shaped like

a crocodile in little green stones, with two red ones for its eyes. I held it up to the light from the window behind the sink. Glancing out, I thought I saw something small and pink in the sky but it turned out to be a smear of Windolene on the glass.

 Matador

For exclusive discounts on Matador titles,
sign up to our occasional newsletter at
troubador.co.uk/bookshop